ZONES

ZONES

A SCIENCE FICTION NOVEL

DAMIEN BRODERICK &

RORY BARNES

THE BORGO PRESS

MMXII

ZONES

FIRST BORGO PRESS EDITION

Published by Wildside Press LLC

www.wildsidebooks.com

ZONES

C O N T E N T S

PROLOGUE

It all seems so long ago. I was only fourteen. I was a bright girl, very bright, and did really well at school, but I was still mixed up, a bit of a mess to tell the truth. My parents had divorced recently, my boyfriend couldn't keep his hands to himself, and I didn't even have a computer. Can anyone who wasn't there believe that? 1995 was a time when nice middle class households like ours usually still had only one phone, a landline of course, often in the hallway. No privacy. No texting. *One* phone!

But it turned out that our phone was special.

Cell phones—mobiles, we called them in Australia in those days—were just coming in. I remember the first one I saw: some guy was walking down the street talking to it. It was about the size of a small brick. And here was this guy in the street with a brick rammed up against his ear and he was talking to it, talking to a brick. He seemed only slightly embarrassed. I just stood and stared, trying not to laugh, as did most of the other pedestrians.

It was an innocent age. The Twin Towers in New York were as solid as concrete and steel could make them. If you wanted to find out a fact, you looked it up—in a book, unless you were a geek with a modem connection to an Internet that had hardly got started by today's standards. I don't think Google had even been launched back then, but I can't be bothered googling it to make sure. It took a solid week for a letter to get from Melbourne to San Francisco and another week for the reply to reach you. Hell, you could exchange two letters a month with your American pen friend. I might have been bright, but I had no idea where Iraq or Afghanistan were. Why should I? I mean, the world's greatest scientists didn't even know that the universe is expanding faster and faster. They thought it was all doomed, billions and billions of years from now, to collapse into a Big Crunch. They didn't know about dark matter and dark energy. They certainly didn't know about time zone resonances. Hey, I was only the second person in all of history to know about that.

So in this innocent time I arrived home one afternoon from the supermarket on my bike. I could hear a phone ringing in the hall instead of vibrating in my pocket, because they didn't do that yet....

MELBOURNE, AUSTRALIA: SATURDAY, 8 APRIL 1995, MIDDAY

The phone is ringing in the hallway. I drop my new mountain bike at the front gate, shove in the key, run inside balancing my bag of groceries, kick the door shut.

It keeps ringing.

Usually I'm there three seconds late so all I hear is David putting the phone down at his end. Maddy says I should call him back but I don't like to push. I have trouble imagining why he goes out with me.

"Hello?"

"Don't hang up," a man says urgently.

"I'm sorry?"

"You sound as if you've been running."

"Who did you wish to speak to? Whom." Youngish, but I don't recognize the voice.

"Sorry, I'll explain all that, just promise me you won't hang up until you've heard what I've got to say."

A charity drive. Or some slick scammer selling a set of Kitchen-ware made from a miracle space-age substance you can safely drop from a great height.

"Look, I nearly busted a carton of eggs getting to this phone. Can you please just tell me who you're trying to reach so I can go and unpack? Do you want my father?"

"Oh. Is that a child I'm speaking to?"

I fume. I'm fourteen, halfway to fifteen.

"Yes, this is a child you're talking to. Could I ask the name of the ill-mannered adult who's asking?"

After a long moment of silence I start to move the handset away from my ear.

"Don't hang up!" he yelps, guessing. "Look, I'm sorry, I'm really sorry, whatever it was I said. You're a teenager, is that right?"

"Dynamite."

"Oh hell, I truly do apologize, the last thing I want to do is upset you. Listen, what's your name?"

"Why should I tell you what my name is? I think you must have the wrong number."

"No," he says fiercely. "No, I have the only number this machine can access. It's not like I can just dial any old number I want."

"What are you talking about?"

"Sorry, look, this isn't just an ordinary phone—I'm using resonant circuits. The whole thing's touch and go. It's a miracle I reached anyone at all."

I'm starting to get the message. This guy is some sort of mobile phone freak. All this hot digital technology: it's breeding a race of try-hards and loonies. Any moment now he's going to tell me he's got his own uplink dish. Maybe his own personal satellite.

But all he adds is, "For God's sake don't hang up. Hear me out. If you like, go and put your carton away safely and then come back, but make sure no one hangs up this phone. I beg you. This is a matter of—"

I grunt, half laughing, and he breaks off. He's had me going, this jerk has actually started to reel me in.

I finish for him, snidely: "—of life and death, I suppose?"

He makes a coughing sound and I can't tell if he is laughing too or just embarrassed by his overstatement.

"Well, maybe not that important, but pretty damn important, believe me. *Do* you believe me? Have I convinced you, O nameless teenager?"

"Why should I believe you, O nameless telephone mugger? I don't know your name and you have a definite advantage, because obviously you already have this number, even if it is the only number your precious little toy can ring up. So you either know my parents' surname from the phone book, or you're calling at random and I really *should* hang up. What's it to be?"

"This is a miracle. It's more than a miracle. You've got a mind like a steel trap. What a stroke of incredible luck. I thought I'd have to try explaining all this to some thick-witted office clerk. What time is it at your end?"

I glance automatically at my digital watch. 12:27 in the afternoon. Then I do a double-take.

"At *my* end? You're telling me this is an international call?"

It can't be, I realize the moment I've spoken. Firstly, there'd been no International Subscriber Dialing bips or operator's instructions. Is it true that they bip at you with ISD calls? I can't remember. Certainly they do with interstate subscriber trunk calls. Second, I'm hearing his reactions too quickly. Speed of light. New York, say, or London, half the time you spend most of your buck garbling over the top of each other's sentences.

That isn't happening. So my invisible caller is not from outside Australia.

Even so, there *are* time zone differences between Western Australia, say, and Melbourne, over here on the East Coast, and then there's daylight saving which some States don't use though we do, so I decide to give him the benefit of the doubt.

"Half past twelve."

"In the afternoon?"

I start to say, "Of course in the afternoon," when he cuts back in, "Oh, sorry, yes, you'd hardly be able to go out at half past twelve at night and pick up a dozen eggs," and I say, "Well I *could*, of course, if I went to a 7-Eleven," and he falls silent.

I think about what we've just told each other and realize there is something majorly fishy afoot. I mean, he is saying he didn't know if he'd called someone in the day or night but the lack of lag in our conversation means he has to be within a few thousand kays of me. None of it adds up.

"My father will be getting home pretty soon," I say, a trifle nervously. "I have to start getting lunch ready, so I think—"

His scream nearly deafens me. "No, please, please, *DON'T HANG UP!* You'll kick yourself if you do. No you won't, because you'll never know what you missed. But if you did know you'd kick yourself. My God, you'd go out and find a thick length of rope and *hang* yourself."

He's starting to sound like the sort of sexual weirdo thrill seeker they warn us about in social-ethics classes, and I'd get absolutely crazy frenzied mad at him except that something in his tone sounds desperate but not *warped* desperate, if you know what I mean. Like a third grade boy I knew in Balmain before we shifted down here to Melbourne, where the weather's boiling hot one minute and drenching wet the next. This kid's father used to beat him with an old-fashioned leather shaving strap or strop or whatever it's called, a thing they used to sharpen their blades on in the days before electric razors and disposable Schicks, anyway this kid used to cop it whenever his old man was in a bad mood which seemed to be most of the time, and he really hated having to go home. The teachers had to shove him out the school gate. That's not such a hot example now that I think about it, but the point is I am starting to feel sympathetic towards this crackpot on the other end of the phone.

"I'll give you five minutes," I say. "Make it good. Any sleaze and I hang up *fast*, and then I dial the cops."

"What? You think I'm—" He laughs rather nicely. "No, if that was my game I'd find a less expensive way than this to go about it. Let me tell you something that might give you an appreciation of what's at stake here. How much do you suppose this call is costing me?"

"Assuming it's a local call, which I will for reasons too boring to go through," I say instantly, "thirty cents. Or less if you're ringing from a private phone. Or nothing if you're using one in an office."

"...Cents?" he says.

"It's more?" I'm skeptical.

"That's Australian cents, is it?"

"Look, what's *wrong* with you?" I yell, getting annoyed. "Do you think we use drachmas in Melbourne? Pesos? Rubles? Telstra was an Australian company last time I looked. Strangely enough, they ask you pay them in Australian cents."

It's just as well Poppa didn't hear this. He hates me talking back to grown-ups in that smart-aleck way, and he'd ground me for the night, which would break my heart because Davy has invited me over to his place to babysit his kid brother and, more to point, watch a video while his folks go to some dinner party.

"Thirty cents," he says as if he can hardly believe his ears. "That's inflation for you. All right, hold on to your hat, nameless teenager. And don't, please don't for the love of Harry, *don't* drop the phone in your amazement and cut me off."

"I never wear hats. I'm holding on with both hands."

"Fifteen thousand pounds a minute this call is costing. Um, that's about thirty thousand dollars."

"Not at today's exchange rate," I say nastily. Show-off. "So you're calling from England, are you? Why isn't there an orbital delay?"

"A *what*?"

"Come on, nameless Englishman, you know perfectly well that an international call has to go to the local exchange and then get bounced up to a satellite in fixed orbit forty thousand kays up and then down again the same distance plus the extra distance around the curve of the Earth, it all adds up. Unless it goes by co-ax cable or optical fiber."

There is a long pause. Then he says, "Is this a boy or a girl I'm talking to?"

That really makes my day.

"Sheesh! Didn't anyone ever *tell* you the difference? What do *you* think?"

"I'm just going to have to keep apologizing, I can tell that much. The difficulty is, I can't see what you look like through this fairly opaque earpiece. Now don't get angry and hang up the phone, but I thought...I *think*...you're a girl."

"Brilliant. I'll make it easier for you in future. There's a rule to apply to these cases, see? The girls have high voices and the boys have deep voices."

He laughs. "It doesn't always work that way. My voice didn't break until I was sixteen. I'm just surprised that a girl would know all that stuff about orbits."

This is insane. The man is trying to win the Blundering Sexist Jackass Award.

Very curtly, I say, "Mister, you still haven't said who you're trying to reach."

"I'm trying to reach the number in your house, which thank heavens I've done." He seems to be breathing rather heavily. "Listen, you said 'satellite,' didn't you? Are there people up there?"

"How should I know? Hang on, there are some Russians in the Mir space station, they seem to like long orbital missions, and that American guy they took up with them."

"Russians and Americans in the same space station!" he says incredulously. "What about the American space program?"

"I don't think there's been a shuttle mission for a few weeks. But they're all working on docking, so they can get Space Station Alpha started. Look, why ask *me* this? Can't you read the paper?"

"The Moon," he says urgently. "What about the Moon?"

"I think your five minutes must be up." My feet are getting numb because of the angle I'm leaning against the table that the phone sits on. "What do you mean, what about the Moon?"

"Are there people up there? A lunar settlement?"

"Are you *nuts* or something? There's nothing up there since they killed off Apollo before I was even born."

"They killed *Apollo*? Wait a minute, this is getting too much for me to take in. Apollo the Greek god?"

I hear Poppa's key in the door.

"Look, I don't find your line of repartee particularly amusing, nameless nerd, and your five minutes ran out at the third beep." Poppa hates me hanging off the phone, as he calls it. "So long, Charlie," I say, and put down the receiver. I think I hear a thin drawn-out scream of anguish and wonder what kind of loony creep the nameless nerd really is.

Poppa catches me taking my hand off the receiver but he doesn't take the chance to nag at me. He smiles, actually, and gives a quick hug as he goes by, loaded down with books and notepads and calculators and his Dictaphone and stuff.

"Hi, Jenny. Get to the supermarket in time?"

"Only just. I haven't unpacked yet."

"Is that your bike sprawled in the street?"

"Yeah, I'm just going."

"You should be more careful, pet. Bikes cost money."

"I had to answer the phone, I could hear it ringing."

I bring the bike into the hallway through the front door and nudge it shut with the heel of my sneaker.

"Not for me, I presume?" He's taking eggs from the carton and putting them one by one into the plastic slots in the top of the fridge door. I'll never understand why he bothers. Why not leave them in the carton? I suppose it conserves space, but we never have all that much food in the fridge now there's just the two of us.

"Don't think so."

"Don't be absurd, Jenny. Either the call was for me or it wasn't."

"It wasn't for either of us."

"Oh. We've been getting a few wrong numbers lately. It must have something to do with the road repairs."

I think of asking Poppa's opinion about the nameless phone freak or at least telling it all to him as a sort of entertaining story but then I notice the Science Show has been on for a quarter of an hour and run for the radio. I hate missing it.

SATURDAY, 8 APRIL, LUNCH

"That was delicious, sweetie. I must eat lunch with you more often."

"I cannot tell a lie," I say, cleaning away the plates. "Papa Giuseppe did it all."

Poppa wipes the last of the flan out of his beard. It's been going gray recently. Tall and rather thin and going gray, a nice person really, but quite vague. "Who?" he says vaguely. "Someone I know, I hope."

"It's a brand of frozen quiche, donkey."

"Rudeness is not attractive, Jenny. Are you saying you cheated?"

"Certainly not! I never told you I'd made it from scratch. That's why I had to rush out to the supermarket at the last minute and miss half the Science Show."

"I thought you went to get eggs."

"You can get eggs anywhere. You can get eggs at the milk bar around the corner. You can get eggs at the 7-Eleven store at half past midnight."

"*I* might be able to," my father says sharply, glancing up from his Awfully Official Papers that are spread out over a third of the kitchen table. Mum would never let him do that. "You, on the other hand, will be tucked up in bed and well asleep by that hour."

I sigh loudly. "*Don't* nag. You know I always get back before curfew."

"Hmph. Scraping in just under the clang of the witching hour. Speaking of which—"

"Ha, very funny."

"Pun unintended, I'm glad to say. Speaking of which, I repeat, whom are you going out with tonight, someone I know, I trust?"

"David. You know him, and you can trust him." Maybe.

"I know David?"

"Poppa, you've only lectured him on the theory of fiscal macro-dynamics or some damned thing every single time he drops in here to—"

"Ease up, Jenny. That David. Nice boy—I think. Does he know how to keep his hands to himself?"

"Poppady!" I'm shocked.

Actually I'm not *terrifically* shocked, because in fact I have to keep warning Davy to do exactly that whenever we sit next to each other in the movies or round at Louise's for a video like *Drugstore Cowboy* the other night, so who knows how I am going to keep him cool while we snuggle up alone together at his folks' place watching something gross? Do I really want to, for that matter? But it is always wise to sound as pure and outraged as possible when your father asks a question like that.

I think he sees through me, though.

"It's a reasonable thing for the parent of a daughter to ask, I believe, especially a daughter whose mother currently declines to sit at the same table with us. I have to do the work for both Hattie and me, after all. Mother and father in one horrible balding bundle." He smiles in self-mockery, which is always a happy thing to see in a grown-up.

"Currently?" I say, quick as a steel trap. The mysterious telephone mugger just won't get out of the back of my mind.

"You know I hope to re-establish cordial relations with Hattie, sweetie."

"Oh, don't be a stuffy old Prof, Prof," I tell him, feeling angry underneath my burst of fond love. "'Cordial'! You still love her, admit it."

"I admit it. But we *are* divorced, after all. Let's change the subject, Jenny. The topic's painful."

"We have to talk it through properly some—"

"Not now." He's avoiding my eye, suddenly. He looks meaningfully at his watch. "I really do have a lot of work to finish. I think I'll take all this stuff into the study. Leave the washing-up, I'll fix it later."

"Poppa!" I shout. I pound on the table. "How can you just stand there and say 'the topic's painful'? I'm *part* of the topic!"

"Later, Jenny. I mean it. I have too much on my plate right now to divert any emotional energy into this sort of draining row."

"I don't want a row, I want to—"

"You're yelling, Jenny. For somebody who doesn't wish to get into a row, you're—"

"Oh damn it," I yell, and slam back my chair and stomp to the front door, where the bell is buzzing.

"Madeleine," I grunt.

"Hi. Would you rather kill me now or should I come back later with witnesses?"

I glare at her. She's doing her retro-Madonna number. The kid's got no taste. For once I agree with my father. Socks in three different luminous colors. Lace around her breasts, which are getting pretty spectacular these days anyway. Ballet tights, dark bracelets from her elbow to her wrist, a wonder she can lift her arms. Metallic woven jacket with bits of silk and satin and leather hanging off it, a bunch of Catholic rosaries around her neck, urchin shoes. God, she looks like a reject from *MTV*. No, that's not fair. Standing there with the early afternoon autumn sunshine blasting through hair that seems to have exploded upwards after her brain went off, she looks like one of the *success* stories from *MTV*.

"My father will flip," I tell her, giggling.

"You got no style, Jenny," Madeleine says, coming in and slamming the door behind her. "Look at you. Worn out jeans, old school sweater, awful shoes, let's face it, and your hair hasn't changed since you were 10. Where's your class? 'Gonna dress you up,'" she sings in a thin little voice, like something out of 1985 or whenever it was, writhing as she bops down the hall. A trailing rosary catches on the handlebar of my bike and almost trips her on her face. She doesn't appreciate my snigger.

"Got any Pepsi?"

"Come upstairs to my room, I've got some in the fridge."

One of my father's lateral thinking breakthroughs was providing me with a small refrigerator of my own, the sort they have in hotel rooms. I keep Cokes and stuff in it, and ice cream and chocolate when it's hot, and he figures this stops me from making a mess in the kitchen. Considering that I am preparing half the food in the house these days, this is pushing his luck.

"Where's the olds? Sorry," she catches my look, "the *old*."

"Downstairs getting some report prepared. 'Nor shall my sword sleep in my hand,' that sort of thing."

"Huh?"

"William Blake or something."

"William who?"

I give up. "A poet."

"Uh. Does he play with a band?"

"Let's start again from the beginning, shall we? Hey, Madeleine, ah *jest lahhhv* yo' clothes."

"Whah, thank yo', babba dorl." She twirls, sending bits spinning outward. She throws herself backwards across my messy bed and tries hard to look like a frame from a video clip. "Music," she cries. "Play music. I'll go crazy if I don't hear music."

I switch on K-Rock but it's doing a retrospective on the era of the Beatles and the Stones or something. Not that I've got anything against John Lennon, or Julian for that matter. No, Julian wasn't one of the Beatles, was he? Anyway, it's Mick Jagger and the Stones who've just been here for their first tour in twenty-three years or whatever it is.

Madeleine finds a Yothu Yindi CD and starts bouncing around the room, humming and pulling faces. "What kind of reports?" she asks, popping a big bubble of gum.

"What kind of reports what?"

"Is he writing? I mean, I never thought about it until just now. What *is* your father?"

"Economist," I mumble. Maybe I'm jealous. That's what it feels like, a nasty little stab. But I couldn't tell you if I am jealous because she's paying attention to Poppa instead of to the fun time *we* are supposed to be having, or because I want to keep Poppa to myself. Having a mind like a steel trap isn't all good times. It hurts. Maybe I just shouldn't worry about it.

Madeleine stops dead and stares at me with her jaw hanging open and the blob of gum stuck to her front teeth.

"Jenny! Your father's a *communist*?"

I fall on the bed laughing, then fall off it laughing. I can't help it. She's such a jerk.

"What did I say?" She's giggling with me, and we are both snorting like fools and pounding our feet on the floor without really knowing why. There is a crabby shout from downstairs to please for the love of God get rid of those damned rhinos or leave me in peace. I choke and cover her mouth with a pillow. She fights me off and whispers hoarsely:

"Tell me true! Is he a communist or what? I won't hold it against him, Helen's father is a bus-driver."

"E*con*omist," I hiss. "Money. You know, that paper stuff we wish we had some of so we could buy a— buy some—" I have to stop. I can't think of anything I want to buy.

"Clothes," Madeleine is saying dreamily, "records, great beads, get our hair done every day, cars, trips to Disneyland and see Braincase playing in New York or Las Vegas or wherever and—"

Downstairs, the phone rings. I think of going down to get it, but decide Poppa's closer. It keeps ringing. I get up and go to the door. By the time I hit the landing he's come out of his study and answers it. He glances up to me.

"Are you the teenager with the mind like a steel trap?"

I stare at him. I haven't told anybody, not even him over lunch.

"Is that Davy?"

"I shouldn't think so, unless his speech has improved markedly. Well come on, don't dawdle, my computer's probably having a melt-down while I loiter here."

I gallop down the stairs. He grimaces and mutters something about damned elephants should have been put out with the rhinos and hands me the receiver.

"Yes?"

"Don't hang up," the voice says.

"You again."

"Oh, if only you knew. If you realized how much sweat and pain and bloody trouble you put us to, doing what you—" His voice cuts off suddenly, as if someone had covered the mouthpiece. A few seconds later he says in a much more controlled tone, "I'm not getting off to a very good start this time either, am I?"

"I don't have the faintest idea." I see Madeleine peering down over the top banister with her eyebrows pushed up into her frizzy blonde hair, doing a question at me. I shrug back and wave my free hand in a circle. I add, "I suppose it depends what you're trying to say and who you think you're saying it to." Whom.

"Who *am* I saying it to? No, hang on, my turn. This is Rod Gianforte. You've never met me, but I guarantee that I'm of sound character and clean in mind and person. Please laugh, that was a friendly self-deprecatory joke."

"Ha ha," I say. I hold the receiver away from my face and stare at it. When I get it back to my ear he's saying, "...tremendously important." The voice takes a deep and shuddering breath. "Listen, nameless teenager, I would beg your indulgence for just three more questions. Think of this as some kind of intelligence test, or a quiz, yes, that's it, like a—"

"What's the prize?"

"The prize? Golly, the prize...it's just about anything you could ask for, I suppose, when you think about it."

He seems so enthralled with this thought that I start to hear a weird sound, in behind him, like a whole room of other people sitting and listening and holding their breaths. "Um, anyway, mysterious teenager, I really would be very grateful if you'd just give me the answers to these three—"

"Jenny," I say, on a sudden impulse.

There is a sound like a wave going out late at night, low tide, gentle but powerful, like a roomful of ghosts brushing through each other.

"Thank you, Jenny. Thank you very much. Now, this is the first question. You will think it sounds strange, crazy, nuts, but please just tell me the simple truth. What is the name of the president of the United States?"

What kind of quiz is this? A quiz for cretins? A test for people who don't know what day it is? Come to think of it, this guy sounds as if he *doesn't* know what day it is. He's already proved he doesn't know what *time* it is.

So I give up trying to analyze his motives and tell him, "Bill Clinton."

"Bill. The informal touch. Okay. Thank you, Jenny. That was great. Now, question two: who were the previous two presidents? Do you understand what I mean by that? In the four years before this president came into office, who was pres—"

I'm really pissed off by his presumption of my ignorance. One of Poppa's snide jokes comes into my head, and I say, "George Bush and before him Bing Crosby." Some sort of awful singer, that's all I know about him, but the reaction is spectacular. I hear this wheezing gasp, then a gulping snort.

"You're joking," the voice says weakly.

"It's Poppa's joke, not mine, but he says the real thing was just as silly."

Very patiently, the voice says, "And who *was* that, dear?"

"You know as well as I do," I snap. "Ronald Reagan, and *what* the hell is all this *about*?"

"Crosby," he says. "Movies. Reagan. Wasn't he in *cowboy* films? I really can't...." He sounds as if he is struggling with a hairball. "Thank you, Jenny. Here's the final question. I'd like you please not to hang up anyway, after you've told me this, but even if you do decide to, give me the answer first. Okay?"

"Fire away," I say. I am getting pretty bored, and Madeleine has gone back inside my bedroom and turned the sound up and she's dancing her disco aerobic steps, and I know Poppa will be out any minute to shout at us. I can do without that, because I want no trouble fouling up my date with David in a few hours.

"Was Kennedy or Nixon the President of the USA?"

"That's the question?"

"Yes. Do you want to hear it again?"

"No. What a dumb-ass question. Is this a trick or what?"

He sounds terribly worried and baffled. "No, Jenny, this is not a trick question. Just tell me, which one was president? Have you ever *heard* of John Fitzgerald Kennedy and Richard M. Nixon, the presidential candidates in—"

"You're driving me crazy," I say. "Of course I've heard of them. In fact I did a social-ethics essay on them last term, 'Camelot and Watergate, a comparison.'"

"Camelot and— Fascinating. My God. Apollo, Camelot, I feel as if I'd fallen into a mythological— Look, Jenny, if you did an essay on them, then think back carefully to this one point. Which one of them became President?" A sort of screech gets into his voice.

"Which one? Which *one*? What do you mean, which one?" I shout at him. "Both of them did. They were both President, you dumbo," and I hang up in his ear, hard.

SATURDAY, 8 APRIL, EVENING

In the middle of all this bizarre stuff, I start getting cramps. Oh great. Maddy's upstairs and I'm feeling weird and uncomfortable but I don't really feel like talking about it to her. Perfect timing for a romantic night with Davy. I was a late starter, Maddy's been getting periods since she was twelve, and it always gives me a lot more trouble than she ever has. Just what you need for a really terrific mood on a night in front of the video. Not that I have any intention of—

So I'm in the bathroom off the hallway when the doorbell buzzes. It could be anyone but since Maddy is already here and bopping around upstairs I know it just has to be David. The only time in his life he's ever been on time. We have one of those once-trendy 1970s' lavatories with pine slats in the door, not that you see in or anything but everyone can hear a good fart if you let rip, not to mention a good plop, and if everyone's halfway through their wine and *coq au vin* down the hallway in the dining room the idea is to pretend that nothing happened. It shows how relaxed you are about the physical reality of the body or something. I am unwrapping a tampon, and the wrapping makes a soft crumpling sound that nobody could hear unless they have their ear jammed up against the door, and I go bright red anyway and just crouch there on the edge of the toilet seat as Poppa opens the front door and lets David in.

So naturally they decide to have a little conversation at the far end of the hallway, while I wait to stop my life's precious fluids running out. From the sounds of traffic it seems like Poppa has the poor boy bailed up in the open doorway. I wish they were both dead, or at least a kilometer down the street.

"Oh, good evening...David," my father says, with that pause while he hunts through the huge list of my known boyfriends. Ha. It's the sort of thing that really puts David at his ease. To make things even better, Poppa adds, "Is it that late already?"

"Hi, Dr. Kanes. I'm not too early, am I?"

"Kane, dear boy," my father chides him. "Like the fellow who slew his brother because he had a birthmark. Or was it the other way about?"

This is not the sort of test David does well at. "Huh?"

"Actually, David, my name is Kane, not Keynes. Don't dawdle, come in. Jenny's upstairs."

I want to yell out "No I'm not, I'm three feet away dying of humiliation," but I would die of humiliation.

"Sorry," Davy says, deeply baffled. "I always thought it was 'Kanes'."

A diesel bus roars by. I smell the fumes. Poppa finally shuts the door. "Actually, no. Keynes was the celebrated economist."

"Aren't you an economist?"

Poppa sighs painfully. "Yes. Not, however, that one."

They lumber past into the kitchen. I flush, wash my hands, and come out calling cheerily, to cover the noisy cistern, "Oh hi. Is that you, Davy?"

None of it fazes that boy. He probably didn't notice. He looks gorgeous, as usual, like Matt Dillon in the video we saw last week at Louise's. I wish I looked like Kelly Lynch, that's all. But why bother trying when you don't? "Hi, Jenny," Davy yells. "Hey, they've got a great double bill on at the Valhalla.... *Back to the Future III* and *Terminator II*."

"Seen 'em. Bor-ing. Come on up. Maddy, stop giggling like a child." She's leaning over the top of the banister and starts down as we start up, after Davy gives me a little squeeze and a light smooch around the mouth that we both make a mess of.

"Hi Maddy."

"Hi David."

Poppa is back in his study. He calls, "I really must put on a turn of speed. Enjoy the film, you three. I'll be back from the lecture by eleven, Genevieve." He puts his head around the door. He's trying to look stern and parental. "Make sure you are too."

"Aw, Poppa, the movies aren't even *out* till then. Midnight?"

He pauses at the front door to muse on the reckless pace of modern life. I try to imagine what *he'd* been doing at midnight 20 or 30 years ago. Getting stoned, probably. Or arrested in a Vietnam demonstration outside some Embassy. Covered in hair. Wearing flares. Erk. "Eleven thirty and not a second later." I pull a face and nod, and he shuts the door behind him. David instantly puts his hand up the back of my sweater and I let it stay for about three seconds, then run up the stairs very fast away from him. I say, "Maddy was just leaving, weren't you Maddy?"

Maddy looks baffled rather than crushed, which I would be. "Huh? I thought we were all going to the Valhalla."

"Nah," Davy says. "I'm babysitting. Jen and I thought we'd look at a video."

"Aw yeah." Madeleine can be very cynical. "I know what you're going to do, you're gunna—" I grab her and start to strangle her, but she says, "—*fool around*, aren't you. You filthy things, you're going to *take off all your*—"

"You hold her down," I say loudly to David, "and I'll put the pillow over her head till she's dead."

"Lively little thing, isn't she? Maybe we should take off all *her*—"

Indignant, we both cry, "*Day*-vid!"

He doesn't look very ashamed of himself. "Just messin' with ya. Hey, is there anything to eat around here?" He opens the fridge and finds my last Mars bar.

"Jenny's been getting these *weird* phone calls."

"Oh yeah? Prob'ly creepy Bertram from the chess club, breathing all his snot down the phone—"

Revolted, we both cry, "Er, *yuck*!"

"We could get a pizza and eat it while we—"

"No pizza," Maddy says, looking for another CD.

"No eating it," I add. "I mean, Maddy, shouldn't you be going home for tea? Your Mum'll be wondering where you are."

"No she won't. I told her I was coming over here to study."

Davy bugs his eyes. "Dressed like *that*?"

"What's wrong with the way I'm dressed, nerd-features? First they tell me to go, then they insult me."

"It's usually the other way round, I know. Hey, actually I *like* your, um, dress. Could we discuss it some other time? Like next winter?"

The poor girl sighs long-sufferingly. "I can take a hint. I know when I'm not wanted. I know blazing passion when I see it. Listen, I read this booklet the other day about safe sex, would you like me to—"

"Let me show you the way to the door, Maddy."

As she leaves, Madeleine sticks her nose in my ear and whispers, "Is this the night? Are you going to Do It?"

I push her onto the footpath. A kid on a skateboard nearly takes her left ankle with him. "Mad, I'm only fourteen," I whisper crossly. "*You're* only fourteen. Davy is only sixteen. Have you been watching too many episodes of *Models, Inc.* or what?"

"Well, Julie Blackford's Done It, and she's in the—"

"Good night, Maddy. Can I come over to your place tomorrow morning?"

"'Course ya can. In fact you hafta *promise* to, especially if you're gunna—"

"Hey Jenny," David yells down the stairs, "where's the *Violator* CD?"

"Under the bed. I'm sick of Braincase. Listen Mad, I've got to go."

"What will you do about those phone calls?"

"Dunno. Tell the phone people, I suppose. Anyway, he hasn't rung back so he's probably got bored. See ya."

"Bye." She bops away down Rathdowne Street, in her own

instant movie, happy as a tick. I shake my head with admiration and go back inside. That girl and I have been through a lot together.

FLASHBACK

Mum and Poppa split up over a year ago. I'd just turned thirteen, and I didn't really know what was going on. Mum went to stay with her sister, my aunt Vicky. I told myself it was because something had gone wrong with Vicky's marriage. I thought Mum had driven up to Ballarat to help her poor older sister Vicky get over some crisis in *her* life. Ha! Well, anyway, that's what I wanted to believe, so that's what I did believe.

Mum and Poppa are great ones for being honest and up front about family matters. Full and frank disclosure and all that. But the truth is: they're not very good at it.

All that time Mum was at Vicky's I thought she was going to come back home. I took it for granted. I mean, wouldn't you? If Mum had gone storming out of the house after a screaming row, if she and Poppa had been throwing plates and glasses at each other, well, then, I'd have had a better idea what was going on. That's how they're supposed to do it. That's what happens on telly. But it was all so civilized that I missed it entirely. Didn't catch on for ages.

Being split-up isn't why I feel so awful though. There are stacks of other kids at school from single-parent families. Only it's mostly their *dads* who've run off, not their mothers. God, you ought to hear their stories, some of them. It'd curl your hair. Actually it hasn't curled mine, but then nothing ever seems to, despite hours down at the hair dresser three months ago when Mum wanted me to look beautiful for Aunt Vicky's twenty-fifth wedding anniversary party. Ha!

Mostly kids won't talk about it, but sometimes, when they know you come from a single-parent family yourself, they talk and talk. Fights, smashed-up furniture, the police at the door so you could die of embarrassment, women's refuges for the mothers and the kids, court orders, the lot. Even broken bones. Lots of bruises they can't hide very well.

Well, it wasn't like that round at our place. No, it was like skating on ice, beautiful and smooth and techno music in the air—and then in one hit you're flat down on the ice with your head buzzing and a nose full of blood. I got home from school one day and Mum was packing her bags, saying she had to go to stay at Vicky's for a few days. "To sort things out," she said. "Marriage is a funny business," she said. "It has its ups and downs," she said.

Poor old Aunt Vicky, I thought, she must be having trouble with uncle Bill. Mind you, the way Mum hugged me and kissed me and told me I was the most precious thing in her life.... I should have realized something was going on. It was as if she was heading off to spend a year in Antarctica.

But I thought she must be clinging to me like that because she was upset about her sister and that rotten no-good uncle Bill. Actually Bill is really an old sweetie and always gives good cash presents at Christmas and on my birthday, even if he is amazingly boring. He worked in provisioning for the Air Force or something equally dreary, never went near the jet fighters.

You can be a real dweeb-head when you don't want to look reality in the face.

But hey, I still don't want to think about the break-up. Maybe I'm a bit like the other kids at school after all, the ones from single-parent families, I hate thinking about it. Not that there's that much to think about, it was so boring, all that on-again off-again stuff for a year. All those visits. All that "talking it over." By the time Maddy and I first saw Mum and this Edward character in Bourke Street, I had come to accept that she and Dad aren't going to live in the same house any more. After a couple of months Mum had come back from Ballarat and moved into a nasty little brick apartment in North Fitzroy, so at least I could go and see her every week. It might seem unusual for the girl to stay behind with the father while the mother goes off by herself, but I was in the middle of exams and besides Mum said she just needed to be completely alone for a while. We assumed that meant a couple of weeks. Then it was a couple of months, including the Christmas holidays. Then a year had gone by. It wasn't as if I never saw her, of course. She wasn't living very far from me and Poppa. All by herself, except when I stayed over for the night. I thought. But I could hardly keep thinking that once she shifted to the creep's place in Kew.

The first time I met Edward the creep it was more or less by mistake.

At that stage, Mum hadn't quite got around to mentioning his name in conversation. So Poppa and I didn't know of his existence. I happened to be in the city with Maddy to see a movie. We were coming out of the cinema complex and there on the other side of the street, across the tram tracks, I see Mum and this guy in a dark suit carrying a briefcase covered in gold catches and combination locks and with this mobile phone in a leather holster clipped to his belt, although I didn't notice that right away. He was explaining something to Mum, who was listening intently, her face turned toward him in a way that made my flesh crawl.

Well, you have to deal with all sorts of people in this world, don't you? Lawyers and accountants and all sorts of creepy wheelers and dealers, especially when you're a woman living by herself because she's walked out on her family, so I didn't instantly think, God, who's Mum's repulsive *friend?* I just thought, Poor thing, she's stuck there having to listen to some wheeler-dealer and be nice to him.

I gave Maddy a nudge. "Hey, Mads, there's my Mum on the other side of the road."

Maddy never misses a chance, so she says, "Well, let's go and cadge a hot chocolate."

We're standing on the curb and yelling at her, but it's Bourke

Street in the late afternoon, and even though the Swanston Mall blocks off most of the city through-traffic there's a tram and a romantic carriage pulled by a lovely old horse with incredibly hairy feet and a few cars that look lost, and Mum doesn't hear us. I still don't think there's anything weird about this. We skip across the road and get clanged at by the tram driver, and by the time we get to the other side Mum and the wheeler-dealer are a bit in front of us with other people getting in the way, and they're walking slowly towards the lights.

"Who's the guy?" Maddy asks. "He looks as if he's loaded."

"Dunno," I say, a bit out of breath. "Never saw him before."

We're hurrying to catch them up and you can tell, from the way Mum keeps leaning her head close to him, that she's having difficulty hearing what the wheeler-dealer's telling her, probably some doubtful scam with money, but her trouble hearing him is pretty much what you'd expect in the middle of the city at that hour, the traffic being what it is and all the other people swarming along, etc. I think to myself, What a nerd, why can't he wait until they're up in his expensive air-conditioned office before he starts explaining about stocks and shares or her income tax deductions, or whatever it is? Why does he have to give his client a hard time by trying to make her listen to this sort of complicated detail in the middle of the rush-hour traffic? All this goes through my head in a flash as we're hurrying to catch up with them, and then Maddy tugs at my arm and pulls me to a stop. I shake off her hand, but she hisses at me in a conspiratorial way.

"What?"

"Let's watch them for a minute."

Maddy's my best friend, but she has some really dumb ideas sometimes. Why do we want to watch the back of Mum's head in Bourke Street while she's consulting with some ill-mannered nerd? I just say impatiently, "Come on, Maddy...," and keep going.

We catch up with them at the corner when the lights go red. I arrive alongside and say, "G'day, Mum." And my mother sort of jumps, and takes a quick step away from the wheeler-dealer, and lets go his arm which I hadn't actually noticed she was holding, and is really surprised to see me.

"Jenny!" she squeaks. "Oh...er...hello, darling. What are you doing here?"

"Been to the movies" I tell her, sneaking a sidelong look at the nerd. "We thought we'd hit on you for a hot chocolate or something. That is, if you haven't got to do something else." It looks by now more as if they're on the way to the nerd's office, rather than having just left it. Anyway, his office would be in Collins Street, wouldn't it, or Williams Street? One of the business zones? But my mother says hello to Maddy, and then says to me, "Oh, what a good idea. Edward and I were just going to have a drink ourselves. I'm sure we can put off the alcohol for a bit. Let's go to The Coffee Place."

Unbelievable. She's been heading off to some *bar* with this nerd. First you go to see them in their office about something and then you have to go to the bar with them. I feel like I'm charging in here to the rescue, saving her from a long boring time with the boozy accountant. Maddy is making some sort of face at me and I don't get it. I grab Mum's left hand, which I *never* do, and clutch onto her. After a moment she pats my hand with her other hand, and smiles in a way that I can only describe as nervous. The light changes and we get swept across Swanston Street and into the Bourke Street bit of the Mall, and while we're getting tugged along by the crowd Mum does these funny formal introductions. Apparently the wheeler-dealer's name is Edward Thing, which is so ridiculous that I almost get a fit of giggles but actually I'm suddenly not all that sure it's funny.

"They keep changing the geography," Mum says brightly to Edward Thing, and he says something about the Mall being an improvement to civic tone and potentially a boost to small business in the CBD, whatever that is, and we end up in The Coffee Place sitting around a little table with black coffee and foamy chocolate and pieces of chocolate to nibble on, and it isn't anything like what I've had in mind—I mean, with this wheeler-dealer, this Thing person being there as well.

"How's your bike?" Mum asks me, so we start talking about this new U-shaped bike-lock I want that's made of duralumin or titanium or something and costs the earth but they keep your bike safely locked to the lamp post, rather than being ridden away by some rotten thief with a pair of bolt cutters. Poppa bought me the Malvern Star mountain bike, but he reckons any old chain and cheap K-Mart padlock is good enough to protect it. He's a bit simple, sometimes, old Poppa. He goes on about how when he was growing up everyone just leaned their bikes against shop windows and came back half a day later and they were still there, just sitting there. And they didn't used to lock the front door, either, just went out for the day and left the place wide open. Of course they didn't have computers or videos in those days to steal, or street junkies either. So he doesn't really understand about bike locks. He thinks if I've got to have one, I can make do with an old padlock and an iron chain. I reckon if I lean on Mum a bit, she might come good for the classy U-shaped unit.

While Mum and I are raving on about bike locks, poor Maddy is left to have a conversation with E. Thing. I can sort of hear them in the background, over Mum's insistence that she isn't at all sure Carlton and Brunswick are good places to ride a bike in the first place, and how Sydney Road and even Lygon Street are death traps even if you're in a car. She seems to be trying to convince me that I'll be run down by some huge inter-state 18-wheeler if I so much as put my front wheel out into the traffic, which is true enough in some places; you'd need to be a suicidal maniac to try to ride a bike down Sydney Road.

"I know, Mum," I say, "but the cool thing about old Melbourne suburbs like Brunswick and Carlton is all the small side streets and back lanes." We've got this excellent networks of back lanes where I live, even if half of them are still cobbled with huge blocks of blue granite and shake you about if you ride fast. "If you know your way around you can avoid all the traffic."

But Mum is ignoring this and starting on about how I should avoid the lanes and only ride down proper streets because of the risk of muggers and perverts and junkies. In fact she's getting so worked up I expect her to start telling me to only ride down the tram tracks in the middle of Sydney Road. So I switch off and try to hear what Maddy and Edward Thing are saying to each other. I wouldn't have thought they'd find anything to say at all, but he's murmuring away in his posh accent and she's lapping it all up.

Edward must have asked Maddy what school she goes to. They always do, don't they, ask you what school you go to?

"North Carlton High," she says.

"Oh? And what's it like?"

What does he think it's like? It's like a school. But Maddy is really polite, for some reason. "It has a *high ethnic component*," she tells him. This is something the Principal's terribly proud of, and they put it in all the promotional leaflets. It doesn't make any difference, the funding in schools like ours keeps getting cut.

"Ah," says Edward, as if this is something very interesting indeed. "I think this is a desirable feature of well-rounded education that my boys have missed out on."

I'll bet they do, I think, the little private school dweebs.

"Although," Edward says carefully, "the place isn't nearly as homogeneous as it was when I was a boy there. There are a couple of very bright Chinese students in Tristan's form."

Maddy says, "Huh, that's nothing. Our form has more boat people than a Hong Kong ferry."

I nearly choke on my chocolate. Mum stops going on about riding down Sydney Road without a police escort and asks me if I'm all right. I say yes, I'm fine, but I do need a better bike lock and Mum says, "Oh, all right, what do they cost?" I tell her the exact price because I checked them out in Bike World the day before, and Mum fishes her check book out of her handbag and starts to write me a personal check. And a phone starts ringing in my ear.

E. Thing hauls his little mobile phone out of its holster and snaps the mouthpiece open and says, "Thring!" into it.

That's exactly what he says. Not "Hello." Not "Edward Thring here." Just "Thring!", like a word in a foreign language. Or as if his name was some famous trade-mark, like "Coke!"

I look at Maddy and Maddy looks at me, and we both have to look away to try to control ourselves. Mum hands me the check, and I'm strangling, trying not to laugh out loud. Mum is gazing at me, rather puzzled. I certainly don't want her to think I'm laughing at her, especially when she's being so nice and buying me a bike lock. I sort of nod my head in the direction of Thring! hoping she's heard him and know that's what's breaking us up. There's all this babble coming from his side of the table: "...don't move until it reaches four point two oh. And we can always cover the deal with the Brazilian perps—"

It's actually pretty bloody hysterical sitting in a coffee lounge at the same table as a tacky loon who's raving that sort of rubbish into a mobile phone. So I push myself away from the table and say, "Look, Mum, thanks for the chocolate and the money and everything, but Maddy and I have to get back to her place to babysit." This is true, but we don't have to be there for two hours. I can't stand to be here for another minute. Mum gives me a perfumey kiss, and says, "See you on the weekend, darling." And Thring! says, "Hold on a minute, Frank," and puts his hand over the mouthpiece on the phone, and turns to me and says, "Lovely meeting you, Jenny. And you, too, er...er...."

"Maddy," my mother says.

"Maddy," Thring! says confidently. Then he looks me in the eye and says, "Jenny, you must meet Tristan one day soon. I'm sure you have a lot in common."

I can barely keep a straight face, so I just wave goodbye and Maddy and I more or less run out of the shop.

Gasping for breath, Maddy and I fall about in the Bourke Street Mall, going, "You should meet Tristan one day" in a posh way. Then Maddy was *being* Tristan, talking with a stuck-up preppy voice: "Oh, hello, I'm Tristan son of Thring! and I've got these awfully frightfully bright Chinese chums in my class. They are called Fu Manchu and Ming the Merciless." I'm saying: "Oh, I say, we've got so much in common!" and "Things were far more homogeneous in my day."

And Maddy says, "We've got a homo genius in our form, he's an Eye-talian called Leonardo da Vinci." Which is pretty good for Maddy. I wouldn't have thought she's even *heard* of Leonardo da Vinci, let alone known he was gay and where he was from. She's more likely to think he's a turtle. So we're falling about and I'm holding on to Maddy to stop myself collapsing in the middle of the late-afternoon Mall when Maddy says, "Jeez, your Mum can pick them."

"Pick what?"

"Boyfriends."

Suddenly I'm cold all over and very, very angry at Maddy. "What are you *talking* about?"

"Oh, come on, Jen. She's got to have some fun."

"Fun? You're bloody mad, Maddy. That's a horrible thing to say."

I feel like bursting out crying. Then I am crying. In the middle of the Bourke Street bloody Mall. I'm just standing there with tears rolling down my face, and my chest heaving as if something solid is stuck in the middle of my lungs. There aren't any cars in this section of Bourke Street, which is just as well, but they let trams through—and one of them is clanging rudely at me to get out of the way. Maddy leads me to a brick bench, and a fat old Greek lady in heavy black shifts along to give us room. I wipe my eyes on my sleeves and say to Maddy, "Sorry. You're probably right. That creep probably is Mum's—"

I can't finish the sentence.

So I stopped being angry at Maddy and became very angry at Mum instead. How *could* she?

SATURDAY, 8 APRIL, NIGHT

Anyway, we go upstairs and hang out in my bedroom. Davy sits on the bed. That could be trouble, so I sit in the chair by my desk. *Chair's* probably not the word. It's more like an ejector seat. The thing is gas-powered and it's got all these controls: height, tilt, swivel, tension, everything. Poppa bought it for me when he started having trouble with *his* back. He said if only he'd had a proper chair when he was a boy, he wouldn't be in such pain now. All those long hours of study, bent over like a paper clip. Yeah, well....

Davy says, "Come over here, Jenny," and pats the bed beside him.

"I want to *talk*, Davy," I tell him carefully.

"Can't you talk over here?" he says and pats the bed again.

Well, why not? We can talk and kiss at the same time—well *almost* at the same time. So we lie there for a bit being friendly. And it is nice having Davy for a friend. Poor Maddy, she's got no one to kiss at the moment. She did have this hulk called Jem once, only he ditched her for a girl called Bo. We all say that Bo is short for Bimbo. Maybe it is. I push Davy away a little bit, not too much, not so he feels rejected, but enough to let me talk. I want to lie in his arms and talk. I feel like talking about true love and what it means. Not soppy *true love*, the real thing. I don't even know if the real thing exists. I don't even know if it's possible for two people to live happily together forever and ever. Mum and Poppa thought it was forever, and look what happened to them. So I try to ease into a conversation with Davy about relationships and love and commitment and all that.

"What do you think about monogamy?" I ask.

"Eh?" His mouth drops open. He's got a lovely mouth, but I don't really like it when he does that, it makes him look a bit... *stupid?*

"You know, only loving one person."

"Jeez, Jen, if you reckon I'm two-timing you, you want to think again."

"No, I don't think that," I say quickly.

"So why ask the question?"

"It's just a question."

"But why ask it? You've got to have a reason."

"No I don't. It's just something we can talk about."

"Eh?" says Davy, but this time closes his mouth.

"Stop saying *Eh?*" I snap, annoyed. "Tell me something about monogamy."

"About *what?*"

"What we're talking about: only loving one person."

"You're the only girl for me, Jen. Honest. I reckon you're heaps cool."

"Look, Davy," I say, "I'm trying to have a talk about an *idea*. It's just the idea of monogamy I want to discuss."

"Jenny, if you want to go out with some other guy, I think you ought to tell me straight. I don't want any bullshitting around the bush."

"Any what?"

"You heard, Jen. Now who's this new dude? It's not that creep Wilco, is it? 'Cause I'm telling you Jen, you can just forget it."

"Hey, Davy," I say, "I'm trying to talk about a, an abstract idea."

"Bloody Wilco's not what I'd call an abstract idea, Jenny. Do you know what he did with Inessa d'Acierno after the last school disco?"

"Oh, do shut up, Davy," I say. "It's just that not all societies use the monogamous model as the ideal for the man-woman relationship. You know, we *are* allowed to *talk* about polygamy and androgyny and that."

"I don't like the sound of those words, Jen. They don't sound like the sort of words I'd like to talk about."

"You don't know what they mean."

"Yes I do, Jenny. You've just told me what they mean. They mean *two-timing. Cheating.*"

I give up. It is easier to kiss Davy than to talk to him. I have to admit it. I like kissing Davy, but I have this vision of sort of lying around and kissing and talking about stuff that really matters. Oh well, you can't have everything.

The phone rings.

"Oh *shit.*"

I run downstairs and gingerly pick up the receiver. "Jenny Kane speaking."

"There's a reward," the man's voice says.

"What reward? You mean money? What for?"

"I mean *big* money. For you."

"Is this some kind of kidnap scam?" To my surprise, I find that I am suddenly quite scared, and I'm glad Davy is upstairs. "Listen," I say, and my hands actually start trembling, like they do in dumb horror stories, "listen, I've got a friend here, my Poppa'll be back soon, I mean he's here too, just don't—"

"Jenny, I thought we'd got past all this rubbish." the voice says briskly. "Have you got a pen or a pencil?"

What? "Of course I have. My mother always has a message pad next to the phone." No mother in the house, but her message pad's still here, very reliable.

"Write this down, Jenny, and everything will be explained. In a few minutes, God and Heisenberg willing, everything will become crystal clear."

Just to annoy him, I say, "You want me to write all that down?"

"No." He sighs the way Poppa sighs when David says something especially dorkish. But he's trying very hard. He keeps it under control. In fact now that I'm relaxing again I'm starting to develop quite a sense of power over him, whoever he is. "I want you to write some numbers down," he is saying, "then some words. A quotation. Okay?"

"Why?"

"Just do it, damn it!"

"You're shouting."

"I'm sorry. Please? Pick up your pen and—"

I snort loudly. "This had better be incredibly good."

"Hey Jenny," David shouts down the stairway, "come on." Loud hip-hop rap starts up behind him, Ice-T. I cover the mouthpiece and call back up the stairs, "It's another one of those calls. He wants me to write down a message."

"Wow." David peers over the banister at me. His hair is falling in one eye. He pounds down the stairs and whispers hoarsely, "Listen, you've got to keep him on the line."

I whisper back, "Why?"

"So they can trace his number and catch him at it."

"David, you nerd! Who can trace him? No one knows he's calling."

"Oh. Hey, I could go next door and ring the cops and get them to—"

"Shh." I put the receiver back against my ear just as the nameless mugger finishes saying something. He adds, "Did you get all that?"

"Sorry, I was talking to someone."

There's a pause. He's trying *so* hard not to be nasty again. "How much did you miss?"

"All of it. Say it again."

"We're going to lose the envelope." It sounds like real anxiety, almost panic, and I don't have the foggiest what he's on about. "All right, Jenny. Write this down: One two two, six two three. Got that?"

"122,623."

"Precisely. Now copy down this quote: 'But now she's in the creek again, that woman made of flame'." After a pause, he asks carefully, "Have you got that?"

"Yes. What's it mean?"

"With any luck you'll understand everything in about two minutes. Put the sheet of paper face down so you can't see what you've written. Okay?"

Davy is peering at my scribbles; I shoo him away. "This makes no sense, you know."

"I'm going to hang up, then you'll get another call. If it works. If Heisenberg is looking down upon us."

"Like atoms? Heisenberg's Principle?" This Rod guy is coming on like an encyclopedia salesman—bits of strange poetry, then bits of physics. It's all an offer on a set of *Britannica*, I suddenly decide, and the thought makes me feel horribly deflated. Then I discount that idea, because here's another one of his really gross sexist remarks:

"My gosh, you're a clever girl. How old did you say you are?"

But maybe it's not sexist. Maybe it's a compliment. I don't suppose David knows about Heisenberg, and he's two years older than me, almost. I decide to give Rod the benefit of the doubt. In fact, I'm beginning to think he's rather cute, in a weird way.

"Fourteen. We did it in Mrs. Levine's accelerated physics class. If you measure an atom's position, you can't tell its speed. Something like that."

"Close enough. Jenny, I think we're going to make history, you and I. My *God*, this is exciting. Right, I'm going to hang up. Don't go away."

And he does. He hangs up in my ear. The disconnect noise starts up, but I stupidly keep saying, "Hello? Hello?"

"What's he saying now?"

"He's hung up."

"Well, put the phone down and come back upstairs. We're wasting valuable time here."

I cradle the receiver, shaking my head and rolling my eyes.

The phone instantly begins ringing. I reach out, and Davy puts his hand over the top of mine, holding the hand piece down.

"Don't answer it. This guy's a whacko."

"He said he'd call back."

"He *must* be a whacko. Listen, let's just—"

I push his hand away. I hate it when people try to boss me about. "Hello, is that you again?"

"Hello, Jenny. Is this my third call to you or my fourth?"

"Oh, for heaven's *sake!*"

"Sorry, it was a stupid question. Let me put it another way. Um, that stuff you just wrote down for me.... You *did* write—?"

"Yes, the number and the—"

He yelps. *"Don't look at it!"*

"I haven't touched it. But I can remember the quote, it said—"

"Don't tell me! This is a test, Jenny. This is a way for me to prove my credentials to you."

"Uh huh." I roll my eyes some more. Davy is going off his face, trying to jam his ear up against the other side of the receiver.

"You're a smart girl, there's obviously some books about the place."

"Half the house is lined with them."

"Right. Great. Now look, this'll sound even crazier than anything I've said yet—"

"That'll be pretty hard to manage."

"Yes, but do it. Number One, get a book with some numbers in it. The telephone book will do, or a table of random numbers if you've got one, or—"

Is he an encyclopedia salesman? Instead of just challenging him, I say cunningly, "How about the *Britannica Yearbook?*"

"Fantastic! Ideal! Get the latest one that's there, and bring it back to the phone. Hang on. While you're there, get another book as well. Any book at all. I want this to be your choice. I want you to *know* that it's your choice. Okay?"

This still doesn't rule my theory out—he could be trying to find out how *recent* our set is, so he can pitch us a more up-to-date one—but I have to admit to myself that the idea is leaky. "Two books. Pure insanity, but okay."

When I put the phone down and start off along the hall, David turns into a dog with two bones. He snatches up the receiver and holds it to his ear, but presumably the guy isn't saying anything so he drops it and rushes after me into Poppa's study.

"What's he want you to do? This guy sounds dangerous, Jen, I really think I should go next door and ring the cops."

I'm rooting around on the lower shelves, breathing hard with pure delight. "Davy, this is getting quite exciting. I don't know what he wants, but it sounds like a sort of quiz. Maybe he works for some, I don't know, some special place that tests you to see if you're smart enough to join them, and then—"

"Oh yes. And then what?"

"I don't know! Get off my case, David. He rang *me*, not you."

"Hey, I'm just trying to help!" He's halfway between hurt and angry. He says petulantly, "Did I know you were gunna chuck a menstrual? I can piss off right now if that's how you feel."

I can feel my face going red. How did he know? Has he been keeping count? My body is betraying me. I'm even more shocked by that thought. No, it's not. There's nothing wrong with my body. I'm a girl becoming a woman. It's a proud thing to be. It's certainly nothing to be ashamed of. I'm so confused I don't know whether to shove him out the door or apologize for my crankiness. But why should I apologize? What have *I* done? Anyway, I realize abruptly, it's just a silly sexist pun, he probably doesn't have a clue. So I say, to placate him and me, "David, don't be like that. Pass me the *Britannica Yearbook*. Second shelf."

He's still sulking. "Get *this* guy to show you a video. You can read encyclopedias together."

"David, *please*." All of a sudden I can't be bothered arguing with him. Silly child pretending to be a man. I take two books down the hall, with David complaining along behind me.

"Hello? I've got them. Now what?"

"You found the *Yearbook*?"

"Right here."

"Which year?"

"The latest one Poppa bought. 1985. But I think all the stuff in it's about 1984, so it's eleven years out of date."

"Eleven years out of date! My aching bones! 1995. Thirty-five years. Oh my God they'll give me the Nobel Prize for this. Jenny."

Davy pulls the phone away from my ear, scowling. "What's he saying?"

I shove him away. "He's going to win the Nobel Prize in the twenty-first century or something. Yes, O Mugger, I can hear you."

"Call me Rod. Open the *Yearbook* anywhere there's statistics, tables of numbers, Gross National Product, that sort of thing."

"Got it. Argentine Employment and Labor, how's that?"

"Don't *tell* me! This has to be a blind test, or you'll never believe me. Close the book and open it again somewhere else, and find, let's say, the number on the top left-hand side of the page. Write it down on the back of the piece of paper you used before."

"You want me to find a number that you couldn't possibly known what it is, is that the test?"

"That's the proof."

"Gotcha. I'll make it the *right*-hand page in that case. Okay, page 901, um, communications, this runs across from the other page anyway, France is the top country, over to the right-hand side, international outgoing—122,623." I lose my voice for a moment, and something creepy happens to my skull and the skin down the back of my arms. Maybe this is what they mean when they talk about your hair standing on end. I clear my throat and say very faintly, "Holy smoke. Isn't that the—?"

"Don't turn the page over!" the guy called Rod bleats. He's having as much trouble breathing as I am, from the sound of it. I can barely see Davy jumping about like a blurry lunatic, wanting to know what's going on. "Open the next book at any page you like," Rod tells me. "No, wait! Is that other person still there? David, you called him?"

"Yes, David's here. How did you *do* that?"

"What do you mean, I'm here?" Davy shouts. He hates to be

left out, but he hates to be brought in. "Does this guy know me? Jeez, Jen, maybe it *is* Creepy, I'll break his bloody—"

"Give him the book," Rod is saying. "Get him to open it at random and write down the line on the top of the left hand page."

"Davy, he says to open this at random."

For a change he stops babbling and grabs the paperback I found on Poppa's special shelf. "*The Penguin Book of Australian Verse.* Yuck, it smells foul. I hate old paperbacks. Is this your Dad's? Hang on, there's a dedication in it. Oh. It's a present from Hattie, 1965. Who's Hattie? One of your father's old girl-friends?"

My stomach jumps. Just more cramps, I tell myself angrily. "It's my mother. Give it back."

"No, just a moment, you want me to find you a random bit. Okay, page 178. Now what?"

"First line. Write it down."

He scribbles, and hands over the sheet. "There you go. Who's Douglas Stewart?"

"I don't know." I turn over my own sheet of memo pad, and put them next to each other, and the cramps really are there, like a jolt of electricity into my abdomen. "Oh my God, David, this is impossible. He told me to write that down before I even got the books out."

"Hey, that's what *I* just wrote down."

Into the phone, I say, "You knew."

"I don't yet." Rod's voice is so tense it could cut the wire to the handset. "Read it to me."

I'm really quite scared, all of a sudden. There's only one explanation for this, and that's crazy. "You can control our minds, can't you?"

He laughs, slightly shrill. "Of course I can't. Just tell me what David wrote down."

"What you read out to me before. 122,623. 'But now she's in the creek again, that woman made of flame.'"

"Sounds like poetry. Poetry to my ears." He's really laughing now, almost giggling. He catches his breath, and I can hear his pen scribbling, I think. "Oh Genevieve, Jenny, you little darling, do you know what we've just done? We've broken the time barrier, that's what we've done. Oh Stockholm, here I come. I'm off to get drunk."

"You sound drunk already. How did you *do* that? Are you a stage magician?"

"Actually I can't afford to get drunk, Jenny." I can almost see him brutally pulling himself together. In a tired, sober tone, he adds, "Hours of work still to be done tonight. I have to recalibrate the bloody machine so I can call you back fifteen minutes ago and read these lovely little items out to you so you'll write them down and be convinced."

"Convinced of *what*?"

"Be convinced, Jenny, that I've done what no one else in all the history of science has ever managed to do."

"Are you *sure* you're not drunk?"

"Drunk with success. Drunk with joy. Farewell, for the moment, young Jenny of 1995."

I go so cold I think I'm going to faint. I clutch at the hall table. "Oh shit. You said 'time barrier,' You wanted to know what year it was. I don't think you're a crazy kook after all. Rod, I think you're calling me from—"

"Thirty-five years distance, Jenny, that's how far away I am from you. Over a third of a century. We're in different time zones, and it's going to make us both rich and famous, even if I do have to cut Dr. McReady in on it."

I snatch at that to keep from falling over. "Who's this Dr. McReady anyway?"

"My supervisor. He's nominally in charge of the research, but he thinks it can't be done."

"I don't think it can be done either." My fright is turning into a fit of the giggles. "Time travel? By *telephone*?"

David grabs my arm and shakes it. His eyes are bugging again. "What? *What* are you saying to the crackpot, Jen?"

"I'm exhausted, kiddo," Rod tells me. I stifle my laughter, and he says, "I'll call back tomorrow, your time."

"All right." Then I remember, and I'm furious at myself for forgetting. "You can't, actually. I spend tomorrow with my mother. Sunday lunch and probably tea."

There's a pause while he takes that in. Fortunately he doesn't pry, or I'd hang up hard in his ear and he can twiddle his thumbs, wherever he is. *When* ever. Finally he says, "Oh. I'll try to tune it in to, say, five o'clock the day after that, will you be home then?"

"Monday. Probably." I don't know whether to take this seriously or not, but an idea occurs to me. God, wouldn't it be wonderful if it were *true*! "Listen, Rod, I think you're doing this all wrong. All you need to do is give me next week's Lotto numbers. Isn't that what you meant by 'big money'? We could make a million bucks if you *really* were from the future."

"The *future*!" David's voice cracks, and I realize he's still here. Disgusted, he says, "You've both flipped!" In almost the same moment Rod says, "The *future*! Jenny, you've got it completely wrong. I'm not ringing you from the future."

I shoosh Davy with my free hand. "You're not? Then what on earth have we been talking ab—"

"October 7, 1960, Jenny. That's when I am. *You're* the one in the future, kiddo. I'm *here*, stuck in the present." And he hangs up.

SUNDAY, 9 APRIL, MORNING

When the phone rings, I snatch it up. "Is this the time machine?"

A startled voice, backed by scratchy rap lyrics, says, "The *what*?"

"Oh." I am horribly disappointed, to my surprise. "Maddy."

"Well pardon me for breathing! But hey, don't keep me in suspense. Did you Do It last night?"

"You've got a one-track mind, Maddy. What is this, *Doogie Howser, M.D.*? No, we did not Do It. If you must know, David stormed off. He said— Can you *believe* this? It was really gross."

"What?"

"He said I was chucking a menstrual."

"Aw, what foul timing."

"That's not why he said it! How would *he* know, anyway?" I've heard girls talking and giggling about this in the school loo, and they reckon boys can *smell* it—but I think that's sexist crap. It's got to be. The very idea gives me sweaty armpits.

"Well, were you or weren't you?"

"As a matter of fact I was. Not chucking one, having one. But that's not—"

"So you *didn't* Do It?"

"*No*! But that's not why. It was that guy on the phone—you know, Rod."

"Jen!" She's agog. Maddy is a true romantic. "Have you met him yet? Have you set up a date? Are you going to Do It?"

I look at my watch instead of tearing my hair out, anything to distract her. "I have to go now, Maddy. I'm expecting him to call back any minute." In fact I can't believe he'll even phone me back on Monday. This is too weird.

"How devastating! My Mysterious Lover the Sex Fiend! You'll be in all the TV news reports. They'll show your mangled body on tomorrow's six o'clock—"

I can't resist that silly girl. Giggling, I say, "You idiot! Look, anyway, that's why I haven't come round. Sorry 'bout that."

"So you have to hang about there just in case he—"

My face is hot. I must learn to control this dumb blushing. "Aw, no, not really. You know. Anyway, I'm off to see Mum soon."

"Yeah. Well, see ya tomorrow at gym. When's your Mum coming over, I haven't seen her for ages?"

"Well, I don't suppose she ever will. I mean, they're *divorced*."

"Jeez. I wish my *Dad* would go away and not come back."

"You wouldn't if it happened." To my amazement and mortification, I start to cry all over again. "It's the worst thing. It's the very worst thing."

"Oh Jenny, I'm sorry, I didn't mean to—"

"It's okay. Got to go now. See ya." Super cheery. No worries.

"Hey, if you're really down you could smoke that joint you bought from Louise that time."

"Too late. I smoked it last week."

Maddy is indignant. So much for sympathy. "You rat! Without me?"

"I nearly hurled. You didn't miss nothing. It just made me feel worse."

"Oh. Well, see ya, then."

"Bye, Mads."

I hang up.

§

In the afternoon, I walk up Lygon St to the tram-stop,

sniffing the pollution and the backyard barbecue odors. I love the autumn, it gives me a chance to crunch through beautiful fallen leaves. I change tram routes in the city, and when the tram to Kew finally arrives I sit staring out through the slightly dusty window and my mind goes into a dazed whiz. None of this can be real. What's my mother doing over here, over the river, among all these snooty brain surgeons and real estate moguls in their shiny expensive cars? Since Mum moved in with the creep I've been to see her every couple of weeks. I still hate going there.

His house looks empty when I trudge up the tasteful path. Just her little blue Honda, the BMW is missing from the garage. Inside the portico, the front door is ajar. When I ring the bell Mum comes brightly out and kisses me carefully, and I go stiff as a board, and we walk through the big house and out into the back garden for our solitary luncheon. There's a tennis court, and the swimming pool is covered so the leaves won't foul the blue, blue water, and trees and bushes everywhere, and some more water glimmering through the greenery.

I want to be a million kays away from here.

I want to be upstairs at home with Davy, pushing his groping hands away.

I want to be in the kitchen making up some fettuccine for Poppa's dinner.

I want my Mum back. It's so hard not to burst out crying. My mouth feels hard and tight.

Mum's feeling the strain, too. "Had enough cake, sweetheart?"

"Plenty."

"One slice! Are you going on a diet again?"

"I'm not an anorexic, Mum." I glare at her, turning the plate around and around. "And I'm not a junkie either." That's what they all think, judging from the telly programs. Stupid adults.

"Good grief, child!" Mum is shocked, or pretends to be. She takes the plate away from me, tidying up, and starts to lug everything inside but changes her mind, sits down opposite me again at the white iron table, knots her fingers. "Jenny, there *is* something we have to talk about."

I twist my mouth about and stare at the molting trees. "Where's What's-His-Face?"

"I wish you wouldn't be so hostile. Edward is visiting his eldest son this afternoon; he's taken Tris with him."

Bitterly, I mumble, "Musical children."

Her eyes are pale blue, and she stares at me. "Why, I don't think 'children' is exactly the word for his sons, except for Tristan, of course, and no, they don't play— Oh, very funny. Musical chairs." I turn away, kicking at the leg of the chair. In a funny voice she says, "No, it's not funny, is it? Not a bit funny." After a moment when we both get something stuck in our throats, she blurts out, "...Sweetheart, darling, please don't be like this. I love you very much, you know."

"How should I know that?"

"I'm your mother! I carried you in my body for nine months. I—"

Oh, really! "We did biology last year, Mum."

"You're upset. I— Now you've got me crying. Oh dear, Jenny, this is awful. I *do* love you, you know."

"I know you do. I love you, too, Mummy. Why don't you just come *home*!"

"It's simply not possible, darling. Not any longer."

"It *is* that simple. Just pack your stuff up, and we'll put it in the car, and drive home to Carlton. You and Poppa don't need to be married to live together." I stand up and grab all the plates and pots of jam and the teapot and stick them in a heap and start into the house, mumbling, "You don't even *like* Kew!"

I get stuck with the wire door, and Mum reaches past and opens it. "When I was your age, Jenny—"

"Aw no. Same old—"

When I look at her, sideways, she's giving this sly grin.

"—there was one thing I absolutely *hated* like poison," she says, "and that was some old fart telling me I wouldn't understand, because I was too young."

"Yeah."

"But it turned out to be true. Not my fault, sweetie, it's the way the world is. Perhaps if I'd never met Edward, or if I hadn't met him when I did, when things were so bad between— Well, who knows, perhaps your father and I might have patched things up. As it is— But there you are, you see, you've got your face all scrunched up like a gargoyle, you *don't know* about adult love, Jenny! Your...your *hormones* aren't old enough to understand."

That's true and not true, and beside the point, and I'm furious all over again. "Look, *you* don't know everything either! I mean, God, I'm just dying to tell you all about this ridiculous thing that happened on the phone yesterday, and Poppa's getting vaguer and vaguer and he's missing you so much, and all you can do is sit there wondering when bloody old boring *Ed*ward is going to get back from his nasty little rotten spoiled brats."

I burst into tears.

Mum takes the lunch things and places them on the bench beside the dishwasher and comes back to put her arms about me. Finally I stop sniveling and she pushes me off a little, gazing very seriously at me. I feel sick, and it's not my period. I know something really foul is going to be said. She says, "We're going to get married, Genevieve. Edward and I are announcing our engagement after Easter."

She didn't say it.

It can't be true.

Say she didn't say it.

Beside myself with fury, I shriek, "You've only just got *divorced*!"

I sob, and my mother holds me against her breast.

"Oh darling," she says. She's not crying. She can't even be bothered to cry. "Oh darling girl."

MONDAY, 10 APRIL,
AFTERNOON

When the phone rings I'm at home alone, waiting right beside it.

"Hello?"

"Jenny?"

"Of course. Who else lives here with a high squeaky girl's voice?"

"Um, yes. Greeting again from 1960."

"I still can't believe it." I can't. Pulling out the extension cable a few inches, I slide down the wall and lounge with my legs straight out across the hall. I really can't.

"Are you free to talk? Getting this thing locked onto the future is like walking a high-wire with a rattlesnake in each hand."

"It's *dangerous*? You mean the phone line might blast fifty thousand amps down my ear or something?"

"Absolutely not." He uses the tone you'd try to calm a dangerous madman with. "I only mean it's very tricky to keep the resonance balanced. Have you worked out yet what I did with the numbers and the quote?"

"Well, unless this whole thing's a major hoax—"

"It's not."

"You'd say that anyway. But if it's not—well, I guess you rang me at like 6:30 the day before yesterday and got me to look up the books and stuff, then I read you what David and I'd written down, and then you—uh, then you hung up and rang me *earlier*, like at 6:15."

"Spot on, kiddo." In a sarcastic tone, he adds, "But isn't that impossible?"

I roll my eyes at an invisible audience. "The whole thing's impossible. But just s'pose it's true—well, after all, you're calling the future. I suppose there's no rule that says your first call can't go to 1995 and your second call to, I dunno, 1975."

I feel quite proud for thinking up this feat of mental gymnastics, but then he dashes it. "That's not strictly true, sadly. I tried that, and it doesn't work. The system crashes."

"What about this Heisenberg junk?" According to Mrs. Levine, it's something to do with, like, in physics you can get away with it but only if no one's looking.

He says it before I can. "See, Jenny, the thing about Heisenberg is that you can cheat a little bit. as long as you do so fast enough that the universe doesn't catch you at it—a small bit of energy cheating for a longish time, a huge bit for a much smaller time. That's quantum theory for you."

"I thought the thing about physics was that you can't cheat. It's not like business rip-offs, it's laws of Nature. That's what my science teacher says."

"A wise man."

"Woman, Nameless Chauvinist. Mrs. Levine."

I'm getting used to these pauses. "I always thought a chauvinist was someone who prized his country over all others."

"Male Chauvinist. Sexist. You know."

"I don't, you see." Rod sounds worn out and despairing. "That's just it. O Brave New World that has such terminological distinctions in it." As if he's muttering to himself. "There could be people with two heads for all I know."

They've been discussing that sort of thing in the papers, we did it in a social-ethics exercise. "Yuck. Transplants. Recombinant DNA."

"See? What's that mean? Oh, DNA—I suppose that's deoxyribonucleic acid, isn't it? What those guys Crick and Watson discovered a few years ago. The, um, Double Helix?"

"It's sort of the secret of life. Everything's coded into it."

"Just keep talking, Jenny." The despair's gone. He is jumping out of his skin, and it makes me buzzy too, just listening to his excitement. A feeling of power, somehow. "My God, this is like having a crystal ball that's focused on next century's textbooks. Have they discovered antigravity yet? Immortality? How about nuclear physics, is there anything smaller than neutrons and protons? Hell's bells, Jenny, I've turned into a babbling loon. You won't have the faintest idea what I'm talking about."

"Quarks."

"Say again? Corks?"

"Quarks. That's what protons and neutrons and mesons are made of."

"I've never heard of it. What's it mean?"

"I could go and get the *Britannica* and read it to you, I suppose."

"In a minute. My head's reeling. Do you know what this implies? We could short-circuit three decades of scientific research. No, wait a minute, we can't. I've thought all this through. It's not on. I have to calm down. Give me a moment, Jenny. My God. Quarks."

He's got me going now, and I'm talking even while I'm thinking. "There's no such thing as antigravity, but there *are* black holes, which is sort of the opposite."

"*Super*gravity? What would that be?"

I've vaguely heard Mrs. Levine talking about something called supergravity, but that's from the Theory of Everything, or something. "Well, if you mean nothing but gravity then that's sort of what black holes are, I think, but supergravity is actually something else in some other theory." But I can't start on that, Rod'll go bananas and expire of frustration. "And there isn't any immortality. My father says people are dying younger, of stress."

"I can understand that. I'm about to flake out on the lab floor myself."

"I saw these old *Back to the Future* movies, Michael J. Fox finds this time machine, it's built into a car, see, and he drives back and his mother falls in love with him. That's just the start, of course."

"They let *children* see films like that?"

"Sure. I mean, nothing *gross* happens."

"Oedipus Sex," Rod mumbles. "Dr. Freud meets H. G. Wells. Ye Gods."

"Anyway, he does this stuff back there in the nineteen-fifties, and his dad turns out different, and they change the future. Is that what you mean?"

It doesn't really sound like it, but Rod says, "Exactly. I've been reading all the science fiction I could get my hands on. They're the only crackpots crazy enough to have given this sort of thing any thought."

"I never read sci fi," I say dismissively. "It's just sexist male fantasies. Apart from Le Guin and a couple of others."

"I haven't heard of him."

Jesus on a stick! "Do you really want me to hang up in your ear? Ursula Le Guin is a *woman*, Bozo."

"Listen, do men do *anything* in your time?"

"Very funny. I don't think you're going to like it here, Nameless Masher, with your attitude."

"I'm not nameless, I'm Rod, remember? That's the big question, you see. Where *am* I in your time—and do I like it?"

"Well, you're not in the Melbourne phone book," I tell him carelessly, flicking the A-L out from its shelf under the table, nudging it back in.

"You already looked?" He sounds impressed, and rightly so.

"Of course I did. I'm the girl with the brain like a steel trap, remember? There's no R. Gianforte."

"Sorry, it'd be H. For Herodotus. Not my idea."

"Doesn't make any difference, there's no Gianforte in all of Melbourne, which is pretty amazing, since they reckon there's more Italians in Melbourne than in the whole of Rome."

"A slight exaggeration. Probably I'm in New York by the 1990s. After all, I'll be incredibly famous."

"Herodotus is Greek, isn't it? Not Italian?"

"They're all wogs, aren't they," he says with a surprising touch of bitterness. "My parents doted on the classics."

I'm embarrassed. "Why will you be famous, Rod?"

"Inventor of the Intertemporal Communicator, what do you think? And maybe the, what was it, the quark." The bitterness has vanished as quickly as it appeared.

It is getting quite dark outside in the street, despite the Monday evening home-from-work cars rushing past. Poppa must be due in any minute. I should get off the line and start some dinner. Rod is loony-tunes, let's face it. I should hang up. But it's a cute fantasy. "If you're the famous inventor of the time machine, how come I've never heard of it?"

That doesn't faze him for a moment. "Different future. That's what I reckon."

I've thought of that one too. "I don't really exist? Is that what you're trying to tell me? Like, you're having a conversation with a figment of your imagination who lives in the future, only it won't happen because I told you about quarks? Rod, I think you've been working too hard."

"I never said it was easy to understand. Look, time isn't just one vast network of links. It must be a sort of...of *cascade*. Every time we make a choice, the world splits into as many versions as there are choices, and—"

I snort. "They used that corny old idea in every third *Star Trek* classic episode."

"What's that?"

"Ancient telly show. They've started re-running it, the Trekkies just keep watching. Also *Doctor Who*. Parallel universes, that's what it's called."

"They stole it from ancient science fiction magazines. But it isn't just fantasy, Jenny. I looked it up. A couple of American physicists worked out all the math. Wheeler and, uh, Everett."

He's not going to give up. I blink, then frown. "So you're saying I live in one of the futures that branch off from yours—"

"Could be millions. Billions."

Slowly, I say, "But that means there's no point in asking me anything, doesn't it? It'll all turn out different anyway."

Again, to my great pleasure, Rod sounds impressed. "That's the risk, of course. We've just got to find a way around it. For example, I doubt that some future universe will suddenly turn out not to be made of quarks, whatever that is."

"I know just the person to ask," I tell him. There's a sizzling sound, and then dead air. Not even beeping. We've been cut off. Or maybe Rod's "lost the resonance." Whatever that means.

Extremely frustrating. I hang up the dead handset, feeling as though I'm stuck in a dream. But the phone doesn't ring again.

TUESDAY, 11 APRIL, AFTERNOON

Mrs. Levine, our science teacher, doesn't really look like a teacher. I don't just mean because she's not that old. Most of the teachers at North Carlton High are only about ten years older than us students, except for the Principal and even she isn't as old as Poppa. It's more the way Mrs. Levine looks and acts, which is a bit like Jennie Garth, you know, Kelly in *Beverly Hills 90210*, only with big boobs like Madeleine's going to have any day now.

And I certainly don't mean you can't have big boobs and still be clever, but Mrs. Levine wears a leather jacket and drives a little red Honda sports car as if she's in the Grand Prix. Plus she's a feminist but she uses her husband's name, which is weird, and she's got a Ph.D. in mathematics even though she just teaches high school science. Mum had an interview with her when I started accelerated physics, and she told Poppa that Mrs. Levine had tried to get a job at the university or in industry, but there just weren't any jobs around anymore because of the recession. So she ended up at North Carlton, which is how come I'm able to stay back after chemistry class and ask her about time travel by telephone.

"Jenny, you look distracted. Having trouble with your homework?"

"No, Mrs. Levine." I stand there in front of her desk while she shuffles assignments into a big shoulder bag made out of leather patches. How do you ask someone about such a crazy thing without sounding as if you're crazy?

"I'm in a bit of a rush, dear. By the way, I was very sorry to hear about your difficulties at home." She gets a sudden gleam in her eye. "Oh, I see. Is it something to do with that?"

"Huh?" I lose my train of thought completely. She is looking at me with sort of sentimental sympathy, and then I get it. Well, what happens at home really is none of her business, so I go sulky and cross. "If you mean my Mum moving to Kew, it's got nothing to do with that at all."

"I see." Mrs. Levine sits down again behind her desk, pushes her long blonde hair back and loops it into a ponytail, and pats the edge of the desk for me to hitch myself up on it. "Look, actually I do have a few moments spare, Jenny. Why don't you just tell me what's on your mind?"

By now I am wishing I'd never started. Outside in the corridor the other kids are banging about, getting their stuff out of the lockers and heading for home. Some jerk is bouncing a basketball off the wall of the corridor, and Mrs. Blakeley yells at him furiously to stop that racket and go home. "Uh, really, it's nothing, Mrs. Levine. Just an idea I had for a story." I stop and look at the open door, wanting to just slide inconspicuously out of it. I've decided to pretend it's a story I'm writing for a midterm project, because I certainly can't just tell her straight out about the phone calls from Rod the mysterious time travelling mugger. "It's sort of a science fiction idea."

Mrs. Levine gazes at me as if she can see something deeper than I'm letting on.

"I see. Let me guess. Something like Mr. Data on *Star Trek: The Next Generation*, who can't really feel anything because he's an android rather than a regular person?"

"Huh?" Where do they *get* these ideas? "No, this is about time. Well, sort of. A way of reaching into the future. Um, well, that's not quite right either, because it's also a way to change the past."

"Ah!" Mrs. Levine looks pleased. "You'd like to alter the past so something that's happened turns out to have happened some other way. Something different and better."

"Yes!" Suddenly I'm glad that I took the risk of talking to her. This could be easier than I'd expected. "Only it looks as if you can't change the past without, um...." It's hard to keep this time-loop stuff straight in my brain, even if it is a brain like a steel trap.

"...without changing the present," Mrs. Levine finishes for me. "That's actually a very mature perception, Jenny. Even when we wish things had turned out otherwise, the fact is that we are the result of everything that's happened to us, even the bad and uncomfortable things. So if we could change the past we would be wiping out part of ourself."

She's gone off the track again, and she's looking ridiculously pleased with herself.

"No, that's not it," I say uneasily, hopping down off the edge of the desk and walking back and forth in little steps. Mr. Ironside the history teacher pauses at the open door, pokes his head in, sees us talking, waves to Mrs. Levine, wanders off. She glances at her wrist, then back to me. "See, in my story it doesn't just change," I explain, "it stops completely. I mean, it never happened."

"But it did happen, Jenny," Mrs. Levine tells me seriously. She leans forward and steeples her fingers. "It did happen whether we like it or not, and the only way forward is to confront that reality and deal with it emotionally. Bottling it up, what we call 'denial,' just makes things worse."

Suddenly I see what she's getting at, and it makes me really furious.

"I'm not talking about moldy old Edward Thing," I snap. "This isn't about my Mum leaving us. I'm talking about a real phone call!" Then I catch myself, and feel my face blushing. "I mean, a phone call in a real story I'm writing. Oh, look, Mrs. Levine, this is hopeless, I've got to go home and start getting the dinner ready, I'm sorry I've wasted your time," and I grab up my bag and books and head for the door, feeling like a complete fool.

Mrs. Levine buzzes across to the door like a sprinter and cuts me off.

"It's all right, dear, it really is," she says, and puts one arm around my shoulders. "Enjoy the Easter weekend, and come and see me whenever you wish to. I'd like very much to hear more about your story. It sounds extremely interesting. Just bear in mind, though, that even in a story we can't change the past. Not really."

"Thanks, Mrs. Levine." I scuttle into the empty corridor and bite at my lower lip. Can't change the past! Tell Rod Gianforte that! Then I start to feel a little buzz of excitement. Maybe he will have got his machine working right again by now. Maybe he'll give me another call through the time zones. Maybe I really will get a chance to change the past.

SATURDAY, 22 APRIL, AFTERNOON

The day Mum gets engaged looks like being a total downer. It's utterly tacky, really, getting engaged at their age. It isn't as if she and Edward haven't both been married before. I mean, you'd think they could just sneak off to the city registry office and quietly get married if they absolutely have to. But that isn't how it's happening. They've decided to get properly engaged, with engagement rings and all the rest of it.

All the rest of it is a party that both Poppa and me have been invited to.

Poppa hasn't been too consistent about the party. He'd actually known Mum was going to get engaged for weeks before she worked up the nerve to tell me about it. So getting the invitation shouldn't have been that much of a shock. But it was. I could see that when he opened the envelope. All the colour drained out of his face and he didn't say anything for a few moments.

"What's up, Poppa?"

He didn't reply, just handed the card to me. We were both invited to help Harriet and Edward celebrate blah blah blah yetch.

Poppa finally said, "Well, it's nice of her to ask me. But I really don't think it would be appropriate for the ex-husband to go to his ex-wife's engagement party.

I agreed with him there. But he said he thought it was necessary for *me* to go. I nearly hit the roof.

"Your mother would be terribly upset if you stayed away."

"Good," I said nastily.

"Now, Jenny," he said. "There's no quarrel between you and your mother. It was me she left. She didn't leave you."

"Then how come I don't live with her?"

"Because it is more convenient.... I mean it is probably better all round.... Look, you can't live with both of us at the same time. And we've lived in this house ever since we moved down from Sydney."

"And this is where I'm staying next Saturday afternoon. Here. In this house. How dare she? How dare she go and get engaged to that man?"

"I'm sure he's very nice."

"No he's not."

"It is hard to be objective in situations like this, but...."

"Look, if you think Edward bloody Thing is a nice man, you go to the engagement party. I'm not."

"Now, Jenny...."

"Don't you *now Jenny* me!"

I burst into tears and ran out of the room. I lay on my bed and wept. I'll say one thing for Poppa: he had enough sense not to try to comfort me until I felt like being comforted. After about an hour I was feeling all lonely and empty inside. He came upstairs then and sat on the end of my bed and we talked some more. He was right, really. Mum will be totally upset if I don't go to her awful engagement party. But I guess she really doesn't want Poppa to come to it. She probably only invited him to show she still cared about him.

In the end I said I'd go as long as I could take a friend. Poppa said he was sure there would be some children...er, um...people my own age. For example, he understood that Edward had a son called Triton or some such.

"Tristan," I said. "He goes to school with some incredibly bright Chinese boys called Fu Manchu and Ming the Merciless."

"Well, then. They might be there as well."

"So if Tristan is going to have his friends there, I'm going to take mine."

"I'm sure you can take *a* friend."

"I'm going to take a whole bunch."

"I don't think that would be very appropriate, but I'm sure Madeleine would be most welcome."

When I phone Maddy, she says she can't come. She has to go to some cousin's place this afternoon. So I decide to take Davy instead, and he moans a bit but finally settles down and says he wouldn't leave me to face the dragons by myself. I really do love that boy.

§

I realize we shouldn't have come the moment we walk in the door. Everyone is dressed up like something out of the Sunday newspaper fashion pages in all these up-themselves clothes. They're standing around sort of like polite zoo animals scoffing pink stuff with bubbles out of silly shaped glasses and jawing at each other. Blab blab blab. And there's a real animal somewhere, barking and bellowing, some huge dog. It sounds as if it's coming from the bowels of the earth, like a tormented spirit.

Mum appears, hugs me tightly and says, "Oh, Jenny I'm so glad you came." And she gives me a kiss and says to Davy, "And you too, sweetheart. It's very nice of you to escort Jenny." Her face is flushed. "I know this sort of do isn't very exciting for young people, but there are one or two others here you'll like. Tristan's around somewhere." She stops talking as if she knows she's fussing too much. "Anyway, Davy, it really is very nice of you to come."

"That's all right, Mrs. Kane," Davy says, and adds with his usual tact, "Jenny said she needed someone to stop her smashing the place up."

This is true, that's just what I *did* tell Davy, but he shouldn't have repeated it. Mum goes a couple of shades paler and laughs nervously.

"Oh, don't worry, Mum," I say. "I promise not to break anything really valuable." I stare around at Edward Thing's ridiculous living room. I suppose it is his living room. Maybe it is his *reception area* or something. There's an awful lot of stuff just asking to be broken: little china figures of milk maids with dopey-looking dudes in matador pants, and silly moo cows with crumpled horns, and a horrible clock with all its inner working parts showing but instead of a pendulum it's got a dweeby-looking girl on a swing bouncing up and down. Mum says, "Come on, then, let's introduce you to Tristan."

That's how Davy and I get dragged across the room to meet this private school nitwit.

He has a blazer and tie on, although it isn't his posh school blazer and tie, it's his *engagement party* blazer and tie. His hair is cut quite short at the back and sides, but flops down over his forehead at the front. And of course there's glasses perched on his nose, like Clark Kent's in *Lois and Clark*. He's standing in a not-really-relaxed way talking to this hunky looking adult.

"This is Tristan," Mum tells us, "and this is his brother, Alain." The hunky adult shakes hands with me and Davy. He is amazingly tanned, with fine lines all over his rather good-looking face, as if he has been left out in the sun all summer. What sort of name's 'Alain', anyway? French probably. He's nattering on in a beautiful voice, absolutely at home in this enormous house with its hideous knickknacks. In the background, like a strange echo, the huge dog is baying and booming. I want to go and look for it and let it out. Obviously it's trapped somewhere. They've probably got the wretched animal tied up for the occasion.

Something bizarre happens. Davy stops scowling at the Persian carpet and really looks at this Alain, and his jaw drops open. I can see his mind do a sort of somersault.

"Alain *Thring*? Weren't you the tactician on the *Pretty Polly*?"

"In the last challenge, yes. You follow the sport?"

I don't have the faintest idea what they're talking about. Mum is looking pleased as punch, obviously grateful that Davy hasn't turned out to be the social disaster she's expected.

"What kind of tactics were you a tactician of?" I ask in a dull voice. "The Gulf War?" Hearing about boys' sports is the last thing on my mind.

"Jenny, don't you get it? This is Alain Thring! He was at Rhode Island for the America's Cup challenge!"

"What's that?"

"The world's greatest yacht race! Hey, this is great! Um, could I have your autograph? Here, on this napkin will do."

I am furious and walk away, leaving them to their stupid boats. The room is crowded with over-dressed rich people I don't know, but it still looks half empty. Up on the walls are these big portraits that I'm sure Mr. Percival our arts teacher would condemn as worthless and without a scintilla of taste or life. Actually they're not so bad. At least you can recognize them as people. I mean, they don't have both eyes on the same side of their heads like some of the stuff old Percival loves to show us on his videos of the great museums of Europe.

One of them shows a young crewman being extremely macho and dashing with a spinnaker line or something on a yacht that's crashing through heaps of waves and foam and sunlight. It's Alain, of course. Another one a bit further along shows a serious young insect wearing a black gown and a square academic hat on his head, and Melbourne University's tower clock looming in the background. Further down there's the dweeb himself, looking about 10 years old. I nearly fall down laughing. An old bird in a pink floral hat looks at me disapprovingly, but I'm choking with laughter, because up there on the wall is little Tristan the wonder boy dressed in a blue satin sailor suit, with ridiculous little suede booties on his feet, tied up neatly with blue satin bows. I almost feel sorry for him. I mean, how would it be to have something as gruesome as that hanging over your head for the rest of your life? I bet he never brings his school friends in here.

"Pretty dreadful, isn't it," someone says. "Poor old Tris says he's going to sneak in here one night and burn it in the fire-place."

I stifle my laughter and look around. It's the young man in the graduation painting, except he's now a few years older. Unlike the sunburned yachting hero, this one is pale and indoorsy. Probably a great disappointment to moldy Edward.

"You must be Genevieve," he says. "I'm Carlos."

"That's Spanish for Charles," I blurt out. "How come none of you lot have ordinary Australian names?"

He takes a sip of orange juice and looks up at the awful picture of young dweebhead. "Mother and Dad travelled rather extensively during the early days of their marriage," he says. "She loved Europe."

"What, so you were born in Spain?"

"Exactly. Or something similar." He smiles to himself.

"And Alain was born in France, and Tristan in...what? Germany?"

"England, actually. Tristan is a very old and romantic name in certain parts of Britain. Tristan and Isolte, you know?"

I don't, but I'm not going to admit that to one of Edward's ghastly grown-up children. Davy is still blathering on to the prize-winning seaman, and Mum has disappeared. Carlos goes back to admiring the portrait of his baby brother. I say, "So where's your mother? I don't suppose she really wants to come and see your father get engaged to someone else."

He gives me a shocked look, then shakes his head slightly, as if he's angry but controlling himself. How dare *he* be angry about it? *I'm* the one who's losing her mother. "I don't find that particularly amusing, Genevieve."

"My name's Jenny. What do you mean, amusing? My Dad's not here either, and I don't think that's very funny either."

Putting down his glass, Carlos says, "Mother died when Tristan was eleven." He pauses and looks hard at me. "Three years ago. Do you mean you didn't know, or are you just naturally rude?"

I can feel myself blushing all the way from the top of my head and across my face and down my chest, and then going tingly. No one has ever said anything about Edward's wife being dead. I just assumed they were divorced, like everyone else. Well, most of the parents I know.

"Sorry," I mumble. "Mum doesn't talk about...you know."

"Her new life? Her husband to be? Her wealthy widower?" Carlos, I see, is extremely angry, and he's no longer making any attempt to disguise the fact. "No, I suppose not. People who trample on the memory of other people might very well not care to mention the details to their own children." He turns on his heel and barges away into the middle of the expensive Kew crowd, while I stand with my mouth open and stare after him.

Someone holds up a crystal glass and taps it with a spoon. Probably a silver spoon, for all I know. It gongs like a beautiful little bell, clear and distinct, cutting through the rhubarb of conversations. The distant dog keeps barking, like an echo from below the floorboards. Why doesn't someone do something about it? A man's voice says jovially, "Testing, testing, two, three. Well now, friends and colleagues, be upstanding, charge your glasses, it's that time of the year," and everyone starts milling about looking for champagne to stick in their long fluted glasses, and they're all smiling and murmuring encouraging things in their silly accents, and then Mum and bloody Edward come out from a side room and step up onto a raised platform covered with rose petals, and Mum is nearly crying with happiness, and hanging on Edward's arm, and I push blindly though the crowd and out the back door into the garden.

I can't stand it!

She's really going to do it.

She's really going to get engaged to this man with children called stupid things like Tristan and Carlos and Alain, and she's going to live here in this horrible big castle of a thing, Thring's Thing, and she won't be my mother any more. Just like Tristan's mother. She won't be there. It'll be like she's dead, only worse, because she's chosen to do it. She's walked away from Poppa and me.

I hate her!

I really hate her!

After a while I stop crying and realize that I'm lost. That's stupid, of course, because how can someone get lost in the back yard of a house in Kew? But there are huge trees and shrubs and stuff everywhere, and I almost fall into some ornamental pond that's got ducks swimming about on it. So I just stand there and look at the silly things and wish I had some bread to throw to them. There's a distant burst of clapping from behind the trees, then some laughter, then even louder clapping. I pick up a lump of wood that's fallen off a gum tree and toss it at the ducks, who kick their webbed feet under the surface and sail off to the other side of the pond.

People are singing "For they are jolly good fellows," and I really feel like throwing up. Where's Davy when I need him,? Inside drinking beer with the bloody yachting hero. I look around, stupidly hoping he might have come out to find me....

...And there's the dweeb, loitering gloomily next to an oak tree, gazing at the ducks—and ignoring my presence as if I'm some sort of unpleasant ghost.

We stand there like two store dummies for a bit. Then, to my absolute astonishment, Tristan reaches up with one hand, still acting as if I'm invisible, and sticks his index finger deep inside his left ear. I try to look as if I'm paying no attention, but it's really gross, he's digging around in his ear hole as if he's trying to scare out an earwig or a cockroach or something that's burrowing into his brain. Then he pulls his hand away, to my relief—and there's an egg between his fingers.

I mean, this is totally impossible. A hen's egg, large size, right out of a packet of twelve, white and perfect and drawn from his ear. It's the best conjuring trick I've ever seen done live. (You see better stuff than that on telly, of course, David Copperfield making the Statue of Liberty vanish, and stuff, but that's all special effects. This is happening in front of my very eyes, and in real time.)

Still not looking at me, or acknowledging my presence in any way, the dweeb crouches down and cracks the egg on an ornamental rock with a sun-dial set into it. I can hear the shell crack. Tristan stands up and starts peeling the shell off this hard-boiled egg that he has pulled out of his ear.

When he's finished peeling the egg he looks at it with satis-
faction and eats it.

Just stuffs it in his mouth and chews it up.

What a pig!

By this time I'm staring blatantly at him without pretending
not to, but he's ignoring me completely. When he's finished
gobbling the huge boiled egg—I can see his lumpy Adams
apple gulping and bobbing in his throat—he opens his hand and
inspects the bits of eggshell. Then he closes his hand, passes the
other hand over it, opens them both—and the eggshell is gone.
He hasn't hidden the shell fragments up his sleeve, or dropped
them on the ground, or stuck them back in his ear. Amazing! He
rubs his empty hands together, shrugs, and still without giving
me the slightest glance walks off silently into the shrubs and
out of sight.

SATURDAY, 22 APRIL, LATE AFTERNOON

When I finally go back inside, the grown-ups are all thronging about half drunk, laughing and chuffing and hooting, and the dog is bellowing underneath the floorboards, though it's harder to hear with all the noise the human animals are making. Davy is still hanging about near the yachting legend. Disgusted, I slide in and grab his arm and give it a tug.

"Oh, hi, Jen. Hey, this is *great!*"

"You're a whole lot of help," I grumble. "I might as well be stuck here by myself."

The boy looks bashful for a moment, which he does rather nicely for such a macho kid. "Well...let's get a Coke and some of that amazing chocolate cake. Have you got an eyeful at the rest of the house yet?"

"Certainly not," I say haughtily. "I never intend to set foot inside this place again, ever, and I don't wish to deign to, um, I certainly won't, er—" but I'm completely lost in my indignant sentence, and Davy looks as if he's ready to burst out laughing but knows it wouldn't be worth his life, so I snort and start again. "And I'm certainly not eating their rotten cake. Look, come outside, that dweeb Tristan just did the most *disgusting* and *amazing* thing, and anyway I think we should find that dog and bring it inside to join the party."

The idea just jumps into my mind out of nowhere. But it's brilliant, and I get goosebumps with delight at the thought of letting some hell-hound loose among the posh show-offs and wheeler-dealers.

"What dog?" asks Davy. The boy is thrown, as he usually is when I change mental direction too fast for him.

"The one making all the racket."

"That's coming from next door, isn't it?"

"I don't think so," I say, dragging him toward the door to the garden. "I think it's tied up under the house somewhere. It's cruel, that's what it is. And it's up to us to set it right."

It doesn't take us long to find that around the side of the house, almost blocked by shrubbery, there's a door leading to the cellar. Davy and I go down half a dozen steps to the door. You can hear the poor dog much more clearly from here, going ape behind it.

"What if it bites?" Davy says nervously. He's usually quite brave. Maybe he's scared of dogs. Maybe he's got a phobia. "It's a guard dog, after all," he says. "It might be fierce."

"No it's not," I tell him, not really convinced myself. "It just wants to get out and join in the fun."

Davy cautiously opens the door and suddenly we're faced by this enormous black and brown Rottweiler in a sort of bunker. It starts frothing and slavering and barking its head off the moment it sees us. Luckily, it has a heavy steel chain attached to its studded collar, with the other end wrapped around the leg of a metal desk. Everywhere I look I see books piled up on shelves made of planks and bricks, piled on top of each other and falling down in heaps, old books with thick covers and hardcover books and stacks of dog-eared paperbacks. Well, they would be dog-eared, wouldn't they, if this is a kennel?

The walls are absolutely covered with heavy metal and grunge posters and basketball posters of truly huge black slam dunkers or whatever they're called, and David Copperfield the stage magician with two beautiful girls in glittery dresses, and a nice big picture of white-haired old Albert Einstein, my favorite scientist. On the desk, above the Rottweiler's huge head, there's a computer monitor with a silly screen saver flashing away on it. No wonder the animal is going ape—locked in a room with a lot of bubbles endlessly popping on a screen.

"I think it's hungry," Davy says, standing well back out of reach of its teeth.

"No reason why it should be. That dish must have half a sheep's carcass in it."

"It's tangled its chain," Davy says, edging toward the bowl full of chopped-up meat. Another bowl has tipped over, and water has spilled from it in a big wet stain on the old carpet. "If I can find a stick or something I might be able to push its lunch over to it. That might calm it down."

On the monitor screen, the bubbles turn into colorful flying toasters flapping their wings. It sounds a bit as if the room has filled up with a flock of military birds flying in formation. At the sound of toasters on the wing, the black and brown dog goes off its face again and drags at its chain, trying to eat the flapping machines on the screen.

"I don't think you should touch its food bowl," I start to say, but Davy has overcome his nervousness and reached forward with a fishing line that he's found in a corner of the den. He misses the edge of the metal bowl and by mistake hooks a lump of meat the size of my head. It flies across the room and lands near the killer captive dog, just out of its reach. I've never heard such a hullabaloo. You'd swear it hadn't eaten for a week. It's staring at the lump of meat and its fangs are gleaming in the fluorescent lights overhead, spit flying every which way, and it makes a mighty straining leap and gets halfway loose.

Unluckily for Davy, its leap sends it straight in his direction.

Davy takes off for the far corner of the room, white as a sheet. The Rottweiler lunges at him, howling with fury, even ignoring the lump of tasty carcass now right under its nose. "Get it away from me," Davy yells. "Help! Help! It's going to tear me to pieces!"

Then I do a really rotten thing. I can't help myself. This temporary kennel is obviously the dweeb's own special cubby-house, and he's left the computer running, so behind that screen saver display there's probably something extremely interesting and tacky. So I leave poor Davy bailed up by the killer dog and take advantage of its distraction. I lean across the desk and very, very carefully nudge the computer's mouse toward me, and hit the button.

The toasters vanish, and the screen fills with words.

"What are you doing?" Davy is screaming. "Jenny! Get help! It's going to kill me!"

"No it's not," I tell him reassuringly. "The chain's still caught. It can't reach you." I'm peering at the screen, which has a file headed *TRISTAN'S CASEBOOK*. A couple of words catch my eye: "Mother" and "Jenny." Davy is bellowing with panic, but I can't help myself, I desperately want to read this diary while I have the chance and I might never get another opportunity to sneak into the egg-conjuring dweeb's underground fortress. But it's hard to concentrate on the screen with all the barking and yelling, and surely someone will come down from the house any minute now. I peer closer and read.

I'm reading so fast I can't make much sense out of Tristan's words, but the general tone of the thing comes over loud and clear: this boy is deeply disturbed. He's as freaked out by his Dad getting engaged to my Mum as I am by Mum getting engaged to his Dad. And he doesn't like me—or he doesn't like the idea of me. Which is deeply unfair, since at the time when he wrote this stuff, he hadn't even met me. There's a bit about "...Hattie probably ran away to get clear of her idiot daughter...." For a minute I'm so angry I could spit. Who does the nerd think he is? *Idiot daughter*! That's *me* he's talking about....

"Jenny!" Davy is yelling from the corner of the room. "Do something! Get someone to come and shoot it." So I drag myself back to reality. It would bloody well serve Tristan right if someone did shoot his beastly dog. The animal is snarling and growling so much I can't think straight.

"You just stay there," I tell Davy, who is even more white-faced and ghostly and ghastly. "I'll get someone."

The room goes a bit darker for a moment, and I realize that Tristan has stepped into the open doorway. "Quiet, Lamb

Chop," he says softly. Instantly, the Rottweiler stops barking and frothing at the mouth, and now it just sort of growls horribly at Davy—all low and menacing. This sounds even more scary than when it was barking its head off. "That'll *do,* Lamb Chop. Lie down."

Davy stays in the corner. He is not breathing very well; he's panting in time with the dog. For a moment the room is full of the sound of synchronized panting, but the dog does as it is told and lies down on the floor, pointing its snout at Davy. There is still no way Davy can get out of the corner without coming in range of the dog.

"That animal ought to be shot," Davy says to Tristan. "It should be put down. It's illegal to own animals that can kill."

"It's illegal to break into other people's private rooms," Tristan says. "And to read their private writing," he says to me. I look back at the screen, but it's full of flying toasters again.

"That's not writing," I say. "That's toasters. And anyway, who are you to call me an idiot? You don't even know me. You're the biggest private school dweeb I've ever seen. Just because you can pull eggs out of people's ears you think you're the ant's pants." I know while I'm talking that I'm sounding a bit hysterical, not cool at all. But I'm furious.

Tristan goes over to the metal desk, turns the computer off without deigning to look at either of us, and starts to untangle the dog's chain. "Don't let it go!" Davy yells.

"He won't eat you," Tristan says. "At least, not unless I tell him to. Come on, Lamb Chop, let's go for a walk." Tristan and the dog leave the bunker. Davy and I look at each other, we both feel the same mixture of fury and embarrassment.

"I'm not staying here any longer," Davy says, "This place sucks."

"Yeah, let's go," I agree.

A lot of guests are milling around on the lawns. Some of them are quite drunk by now. The noise level has risen still further and people are starting to shout at each other. Mum is deep in conversation with Alain and a couple of other people. I start to walk over to her to say goodbye, but then I think better of it. I grab Davy's arm and we leave by the front gate. While we are standing at the tram stop we see Tristan and the Rottweiler walking towards us on the other side of the road. I don't know if Tristan even sees us. He has his head down and might even be muttering to himself. The dog seems to be towing him along. Tristan doesn't look very happy.

"Jeez, I'd like to sock him one," Davy says.

For a couple of seconds I silently agree with Davy, but then the sight of Tristan mooching unhappily along suddenly drives all the anger out of me. "Oh, he's probably all right," I say.

"Aw, what?" Davy says. "He's a prize dork. If it wasn't for that damn dog...."

"He hates the engagement as much I do," I say. "He's in exactly the same position. He doesn't want his dad to marry someone else...."

"Jeez, Jenny. His dad is a real drag. Your Mum's one of the nicest people I know...."

"Yeah," I hear myself say, "That's what it looks like to us. But from Tristan's point of view...."

"You wouldn't want to see anything from that nerd's point of view."

But I can't help myself. All of a sudden, sad and lonely as I feel, I can see it all too easily from Tristan's point of view. And I suspect he sees it from mine.

TRISTAN'S CASEBOOK:
April 22

The subject is a young woman of fourteen years of age. She manifests some of the uncertainties usual in adolescents of that age. An Intelligence Quotient considerably in excess of the statistical mean helps compensate for those gaucheries that occasionally limit her world view. The subject comes from a broken home, her father having proved incapable of retaining the affections of her mother Hattie. It can be assumed that this insecurity explains her choice of "boyfriend," a lumpen young man of considerably lesser IQ, who never-the-less provides a crude supportive friendship.

The present writer is involved with the subject because the subject's mother is about to marry his father. An interesting interaction took place at the "engagement party" that celebrated this upcoming union. The subject and her "boyfriend" were poking about in a reprehensible manner in the present writer's private domains and were "bailed up" by the present writer's faithful hound "Lamb Chop."

When the present writer's father heard of this event and the attendant "bad-feeling" that resulted, he insisted that a reconciliation take place and suggested a meeting on neutral ground—for instance a video arcade. It is a measure of the father's sincerity in this regard that he is prepared to bankroll the whole exercise and has already pressed a number of monetary funds on the present writer.

SUNDAY, 23 APRIL, AFTERNOON

The phone is ringing while I'm fumbling with the key. I think it must be Rod so I fumble harder. The phone keeps pulsing away behind the front door. I get it open and pounce on the phone.

"Rod?" I say, "Is that you?"

"Um, no," says a different voice, "I am afraid it's only me."

For a moment I'm completely confused. I know the voice but I can't picture its owner. Then I suddenly know only too well. "Oh, it's you, is it?" I say, quite coldly.

"Well, I'm sorry I'm not Rod," Tristan says. "Rod must be some hunk."

"Drop dead."

"Charming," Tristan says.

"Look, what is this? Have you just rung me up to tell me I'm charming? Because if you have—"

"Don't be like that, Jenny. We are going to be brother and sister, so we might as well learn to get along together."

"I don't see why. And as for this brother-sister thing, I believe it's got something to do with having the same parents, not just having a mother who's run away from home and shacked up with some no-hoper. Even if they do get engaged in some stupid ceremony with a lot of dead rose petals and people getting drunk all over the garden...." And then I'm crying. I simply can't believe it, but it's happening. I'm on the phone crying to Tristan.

"I know it hurts, Jenny," Tristan says. "It hurts me too.

There's no point in fighting."

He's right, actually, but I still feel angry and upset. I stop crying and say, "Yeah, well, all right. Anyway, why did you ring me up? I don't think we've got anything to say to each other."

"Well, maybe we haven't. But we don't know that until we've talked to each other."

"We're talking now, aren't we?"

"I think we should meet somewhere. There are limits to what you can say on the phone."

But in fact we talk some more on the phone and I start to feel a bit less angry and then Tristan suggests we meet at the Time Zone arcade in the city. I've never been there. I don't think Poppa would consider it the sort of place I ought to go to. I'm sure he thinks it's full of dope peddlers. Maybe it is—but I wouldn't mind checking it out. I say, "Oh, all right, but I'm bringing a friend."

Tristan says, "Davy? Or Rod?"

I sort of giggle. "I couldn't bring Rod."

"Why not? You seemed eager enough to talk to him just now."

"Yeah," I say, "But he lives in 1960."

There's a moment of baffled silence. "I don't get you."

"It doesn't matter," I say. "I'll meet you at the Arcade tomorrow after school. I'll bring Davy and maybe my friend Maddy. See you."

I go off to the kitchen to grab a bowl of corn flakes. The funny thing is: I feel quite happy. I'm quite looking forward to meeting Tristan again. After I've finished the corn flakes I phone Maddy. She's really pleased at the idea of checking out Tristan, not to mention the Arcade. She's never been there either. Then I ring Davy. He's not so keen on meeting Tristan again, to say the least. But I tell him that Maddy and I are going anyway, so he says he'll come too, just to add a bit of support. Big deal.

MONDAY, 24 APRIL, AFTERNOON

After school, Maddy and Davy and I get the tram into town. Davy starts telling Maddy about Tristan. "He's got these real small piggy eyes," Davy says. "And these glasses made out of the ends of beer bottles. And he wears these ratty jackets with thirty five pens sticking out of the pockets and he's got braces on his teeth made out of paper clips."

"What about his really bright Chinese friends?" Maddy says.

"He hasn't got any friends," Davy says. "They don't even let him in the house. He has to live in the cellar with the dog."

Maddy is giggling and falling about and Davy is enjoying himself and has his arm around my shoulder. I shrug his arm off and say, "He doesn't live down there. That's just his den."

"How do you know?" Davy says.

"There was no bed in there, you dope."

Maddy says, "He probably sleeps on the floor with the dog."

Davy says, "The dog's got braces on its teeth as well, only they're made of barbed wire."

Maddy giggles. I say to Davy, "You weren't being such a smart-arse when the dog bailed you up." I'm getting really cross with my friends. In fact I'm half wishing I'd left them at home and arranged to meet Tristan by myself. I move Davy's hand off my leg. "This is our stop," I say, "and about time too."

"What's eating you?" Davy says. "Fallen for dweeb-head, have you?"

"He's going to be my brother. So shut up."

We jump down onto the road and the tram goes rattling off to St Kilda. Maddy says to Davy: "I bet he's wearing his school uniform."

Davy says, "St. Dweeb's Scottish Academy for Young Nerds."

I'm getting really pissed off with the pair of them. "Just shut up," I yell at them. "Or go away! I'll go and meet Tristan by myself."

"All right, Jenny," Davy says as we are crossing the road to the Arcade. "Lighten up a bit. We're just joking." He puts his arm around my waist but I do a side step and get free.

Maddy just says, "Sorry, Jenny.'

§

There's a security man on the door of the Arcade. A big guy with a huge stomach and a two-way radio hanging off his belt. We slink past him. Inside everything is flashing and techno music is blasting from the speakers. I suddenly realize this is hardly the place to have a conversation with Tristan or anybody else. But maybe that's a good thing—maybe we can sort of get to know each other a bit without too much talking. And given the way Maddy and Davy are carrying on, maybe a no-conversation rule would be a blessing. We're standing there, looking around the Arcade, wondering if Tristan is already here, inside one of the racing cars, perhaps. Or landing on the moon. Suddenly there's a tap on my shoulder and I feel a light kiss on my cheek.

"Hello, Jenny," Tristan says. "I'm glad you made it."

I shoot a quick glance at Davy. He looks like he's ready to start a fight. I don't think he thinks anybody but him is allowed to kiss me.

"Oh hello," I say to Tristan and give him a quick peck on his cheek. He's not wearing all his proper school uniform. He's got an old parachute jump-suit top on that says PROPERTY OF NEW YORK YANKEES on it. You can't see the shirt under-neath, but his pants are the uniform pants from hell. At least he's taken his shiny brown school shoes off and put on a decent pair of high tops.

Tristan reaches into a pocket and pulls out a handful of tokens. He says, "Here, my Dad's bankrolling this. It's to make up for Lamb Chop."

"It's all right," I say. My pride is hurt. "We've got the odd dollar between us."

Tristan insists. "You can buy us all an iced coffee later, if you want to. But we might as well use up Dad's money in here."

"Too right," says Davy. "After what that animal did to me."

"It just growled at you," I tell him sharply. "But, okay, we use up Edward's tokens in here and I'm paying for the coffee." I'm not too keen on the idea of accepting Edward bloody Thring's dough, but Tristan has all ready gone and bought the tokens. So we might as well use them up.

I start playing Virtua Fighter with Davy. On another machine, Maddy plays the same thing with Tristan. Davy's too good for me. After a couple of rounds I collapse in a heap. We both wander over to where Maddy and Tristan are still hard at it.

They've attracted a small group of onlookers—boys mainly, all wearing their baseball caps the wrong way round. It would make Poppa freak. Maddy is being Wanda the girl ninja. She's beating the stuffing out of Tristan's character.

On the big screen, Wanda goes twirling through the air, kicking and punching and somersaulting all at once. Maddy's fingers are thrashing the controls like a drum soloist cracking a psycho. Wanda hurtles through space and kicks Tristan's character in the head. The sound is like a thick piece of timber cracking. He goes spinning backwards, smashes flat on the ground. The ground vibrates, and not just on the screen. There's a sound like a train crash as Wanda lands on top of her opponent and stomps his face. She leaps back and stands like a traffic cop with one arm outstretched. She's got her hair in a pony tail but with a red head band covered in Japanese writing. Wanda wears a black bra, baggy pants and big lace-up boots, and I have this sudden strong picture of what Madeleine's next outfit will be.

Tristan rattles his controls and his character comes flying straight off the ground, throws a vicious kick at Wanda, but Wanda is no longer there, Maddy has already dropped her to the ground and rolled her away, cool as a cucumber. Tristan's character kicks air. I cheer. Tristan mutters something and hits his controls even harder. Wanda bounds up and knocks her opponent flat. Tristan goes ape, but it is too late. The screen announces that Wanda is the winner with 5,897,876 more points than her opponent.

They chose new characters and play each other again while Davy and I watch. In this game Maddy is a fire-breathing robot with almost no head. But the lack of brains is no problem. The contest is still hopelessly uneven. Maddy *flattens* Tristan. I watch Maddy's face as she plays. It's hard to recognize the girl. She's all concentration. Tristan flails around hopelessly. I try to judge what he's thinking, but it is impossible. The game finishes with Maddy winning by more than seven million points.

Tristan shrugs, and turns away from the board. "Let's see who's the better shot." He points at a video machine with a couple of hand guns attached to it.

"Sure," Maddy says.

Davy and I watch from a distance as Tristan and Maddy push through the crowd to the machine. Tristan starts to show Maddy what to do. She positions herself like a telly cop, holding the gun two-handed, pointing at the screen, while Tristan sort of stands close behind her with one arm over her shoulder, showing her some of the finer points to the art of pulling a trigger. With his other hand he waves his own gun around. He says something, his mouth about two centimeters from Maddy's ear. Maddy laughs.

Beside me, Davy says in amazement, "Jeez, Jen, that guy's coming on all heavy with Mad."

I look at him with wide eyes. "No kidding?"

"Do you reckon we should rescue her?"

"Get real, Davy," I say. "Does she look like she wants to be rescued?"

Tristan sticks a token in the machine and the pair of them stand there side by side like two tough but sensitive cops in the *Blue*, firing at the screen, except this isn't brutal New York, it's desert warfare. Great waves of tanks are careening towards them over hectares of sand dunes. Every time one of the shooters hits a tank, it explodes with a roar. Davy and I shove through, stand just behind Maddy and Tristan. It's a bit hard to tell who's destroying the most tanks just by looking at the fire-fight, but in the top corners of the screen the scores go rolling up.

We wander around the different machines, play a bit more. There's one last epic struggle between Maddy and Tristan, driving racing cars on a dangerous circuit. Maddy loses. Tristan is overjoyed, his face flushed. I'm furious with Maddy, because I suspect she lost on purpose. I'm *sure* she lost on purpose. She did it just to butter-up Tristan's ego. But I don't say anything.

It's getting dark when we leave the arcade and straggle down the street to a deli with a few tables. Sitting there drinking iced coffee through a straw, it seems to me that the result of this little exercise in reconciliation is a beautiful friendship between Tristan and Maddy. There they are, on the other side of the table from me and Davy, slurping away through their straws with their shoulders almost touching. They're doing a move-by-move analysis of one of the games they've just played.

You could put the pair of them in a couple of matching blazers and put them on telly. If it was football they were discussing rather than Virtua Fighter, they'd be just right for *Football Inquest* or *Match of the Day*. Davy tries to talk to me about the games we played, but I can't remember them. I like playing computer games every now and then. But afterwards they're just a blur. They're not something you need to discuss. So I try to get a conversation going about something interesting.

"Have you ever taken Lamb Chop to an obedience school?" I say to Tristan. He doesn't answer, he just keeps on yakking to Maddy. "Hey! Tristan, about your dog," I say a bit louder, "have you thought of getting him trained?"

"He *is* trained," Tristan says without taking his eyes off

Maddy. She was looking at him, too.

"Trained to kill," Davy says with feeling.

"Only on command," says Tristan. "Would you like to meet my dog?" he says to Maddy.

"I'm told it's got barbed wire teeth," Maddy says.

"It's as meek as a lamb...."

"...Chop!" says Davy, making a karate chop with his hand.

For Davy, this is a pretty good joke. I laugh and lean on his shoulder a bit. Davy lets his arm slide round my waist and under my sweater. I let him keep it there, on my bare skin, for at least ten seconds. Over the other side of the table Maddy and Tristan have started to discuss their favorite films. I groan inwardly. When people start to discuss movies like that, they usually end up going to see one together. I get the impression me and Davy aren't going to be invited to go along too.

§

On the tram home, I say to Maddy, "Get his number?"

"What number?"

"Tristan's telephone number, you idiot."

"Jeez," Davy says, "what would Mad want with Dweeb-head's phone number?" He can be a bit thick at times, Davy.

Maddy blushes. She doesn't usually blush, my friend Maddy, but she does now. "He said to get it off you," she says.

"Haven't got it," I say. "And it's not in the book. You'll never see him again."

"Yes you have, Jen," says Davy. "It's the number you use to ring up your Mum now she's moved in." Davy is a big help at times. Suddenly I'm reminded that Mum is now living in the same house as Edward Thring. She's living in the same house as Tristan. When Mum gets up in the morning, it's Tristan she has breakfast with. Not me. It's Tristan she sees off to school. Not me. Suddenly I feel angry at Tristan and Maddy. I don't feel like teasing Maddy anymore. I sit there on the rocking, clattering tram wishing I'd never agreed to Tristan's big reconciliation scene. All that happens is Tristan and Maddy start behaving like soggy biscuits and I end up feeling miserable about Mum. Davy puts his arm round me. I lean on his shoulder and close my eyes.

WEDNESDAY, 26 APRIL, AFTERNOON

When Rod finally "retrieves the resonance envelope" and gets through to me again, I hit him straight off with my great new theory of what to do with time travel by phone and how to make pots of money without damaging his system. Even though Mrs. Levine was a complete washout, I've been figuring this out for more than two weeks, including the Easter school break. Rod's not impressed, though, and I try hard to work out why he doesn't think my plan would work.

"So you figure even if I gave you all last Saturday's Lotto numbers it wouldn't mean a thing, because I'm living in a future where you didn't win?"

"No, that's not the problem," he says wearily. "Look, suppose time is actually very conservative—" He pauses, lost for words.

"You mean it's always locked on to pretty much the same track?"

"Exactly. Maybe time has immense inertia, like a massive boulder that's thundering down a hill. Once it starts, it's very hard to stop. You can't even divert its path without applying a huge sideways force. And if you stand in the way, you'll just get crushed."

"You mean we can't change what's going to happen? That's a horrible idea!"

"I agree," Rod says bleakly. "It's even got a name—'predestination.' But that's not quite it. Here's a better way to picture it: suppose time is like a vast elastic band. You can deform it, even stretch it a bit, but sooner or later it's going to bounce back to where it was. And crush you like a bug."

I'm horrified by all this doom and gloom and bug-crushing. "Look, lighten up, Rod. That's just a theory, isn't it? We'll never know unless we try it."

He sighs. "Okay, you give me the winner of the Melbourne Cup for 1960, which is going to be run in about a month from now. I place a bet on it. What happens?"

"You win a fortune and go to New York." And, I think happily, I take half.

"No, I've worked this through carefully. Even if some long-shot wins at 100 to one, I can't win a million quid without putting down ten thousand pounds. How can I get my hands on that sort of money?"

"All right." It doesn't seem such a lot, but I suppose there's inflation. And anyway lots of people run up huge debts. Couldn't he harass his bank manager or something? "What about this? I could tell you the Melbourne Cup winners for *ten* years. Then you just keep putting your winnings back on each time. Wouldn't that grow by compound interest or whatever it's called without anyone noticing?"

"Forget the Melbourne Cup. There are races every week." Rod doesn't sound as enthusiastic as I'd expected.

"I'll help," I tell him. "I could probably research the results in the State Library where they keep all the old newspapers. Or just use a search engine of Dad's computer—although he hates me touching it."

"Your father has a *computer?* Oh, you mean at work."

"No, here at home. I keep asking him to get me one, but he says it will stunt my mental growth."

Another one of those pauses. "Okay. Forget I asked. But anyway, look. I start off betting ten pounds, say, or 100 pounds. Hell, I'll get a double mortgage and put a thousand down. You're right, it wouldn't take all that long to build up a decent stake. But Jenny, *then what?*"

Huh? "You're incredibly rich and you send half to me," I say, shaking my head at his slowness, "and you go off to New York so your name isn't in the book."

"Jenny, I'd be in *all the papers*. Believe me. The fabulous gambler who never goes wrong. The mysterious punter with the Italian surname. They'd arrest me for mopery and dopery. Gangsters who fix horse races would bump me off in the dark of the night. You would already know my name for sure, kiddo. Famous mysterious Mafia victim of the early nineteen-sixties."

"But that didn't happen. As far as I know." But after all, it would've been years ago. How many dead gangsters do I know of? Or victims.

"Precisely. Why not? Because it didn't work. Or I didn't do it."

"You were smarter than that," I suggest, thinking fast. "You got all your friends to place the bets for you. You set up a company to do it. You waited until Lotto started up and made a fortune in one go during a Golden Lotto draw."

"What *is* this Lotto you keep talking about?"

I've never bought a ticket, because Poppa says the odds are ludicrous and who am I to disagree with an economist who has all the official results in a official State government computer file? Maddy lives for the Saturday draw, but she's never even won a minor division. "You tell them which six numbers out of forty-five. If you get a first division prize, you win millions. Well, unless twenty other people share it that week."

"Hmm." The line hums distantly while he muses. "Same problem. Why haven't I been heard of? Or have I?"

"No. I checked. Unless you won under another name."

"You *checked*?"

"This is Miss Smarty Pants here, Rod. Poppa did some sort of audit for the government a while back so he has all the official records in his desktop computer. I sneaked a look this morning. He doesn't know I know his password. No Gianforte."

"I knew it. I really knew it." He doesn't sound very happy at being right all the time. "It's built into the theory. I was just trying to hide the grim truth from myself."

"What grim truth? You don't know we can't use this thing."

"'We'? You're getting awfully pushy suddenly."

I smirk, but he can't see through the phone. "So sorry. I'll just hang up and let you get back to your—"

"*Don't hang up!* If you had any idea what I have to go through to get this system into resonance...."

"My ear is getting sore." But of course I don't hang up. I'd rather die at this point. I'm starting to get worried that Poppa will march in and trip over my legs and *make* me hang up.

"Can you check for Dr. McReady's number?"

"He's not in the book either." Of course that was the second thing I searched for, after his own name. "But look, Rod, if I give you this address, you could leave a message for me, something with your own 1995 address."

"No, no, no. Don't you see? *That's the basic paradox.* We don't know how much information can be sent back and forth through time without compromising the resonance. If I know the exact address where you live, I might inadvertently do something in the next twenty-five years that prevents your family from living there. Even knowing your phone number might destroy the—"

"You *have* my number. How else could you ring this phone?"

"Oh Jenny, it's so complicated. I *don't* have your number. That's not how this thing works. See, the mathematics of electromagnetism gives two solutions to each equation, what we call the 'retarded' wave and the 'advanced' wave."

"I'll be the advanced wave. You can be the retarded one."

"Ha ha. In physics it's the other way round. Look, toss a pebble into a pool—"

"I'd get the carpet wet." I stand up and wiggle my toes. It's quite dark outside now.

"There's a splash. The ripples go out to the edge. Then they bounce off the sides of the pool and flow inwards. Think of the inwards ripples as going backwards in time. They're 'advanced' waves."

Suddenly I see it! It's beautiful, like a moiré laser experiment. "And you get interference patterns where they meet?

Pretty crisscrosses."

"Right."

"Like holograms."

"Like what?"

"Three-dimensional pictures. You use the interference patterns of laser light—"

"I don't think I want to hear this. It makes me feel like a caveman peering through a crack at an atomic pile."

"A what?"

He's incredulous. "You don't have atomic power anymore?"

"Oh. A nuclear reactor?"

"Nuclear reactions are what happen inside a pile, so I suppose so."

"We don't use power reactors in Australia. There's too much radioactive waste, and they're way too dangerous. Didn't they know that in your time?"

"No, sweetheart," Rod says sadly, "there's a lot we don't know in my time."

SATURDAY, 29 APRIL, AFTERNOON

I get off the tram and make my way to Tristan's house. This will be the first time I've been alone with him. Mum and Edward have gone away for the weekend, they've booked themselves into an old done-up, deconsecrated church in the bush. You get to stay in this church and eat and drink and sleep and listen to the bell-birds and apparently you become spiritually renewed. Tristan is all by himself for two days. Mum said on the phone that he'd insisted he was old enough to look after himself. I suppose he is. I'm not sure what to expect from my visit. I don't any longer think that Tristan's the nerd he makes himself out to be in company. I'm interested to see if I can talk to him by myself. When he answers the doorbell, it seems he's surprised I'm alone.

"Where's Maddy?" he asks, a bit grumpily.

"I don't go everywhere with Maddy," I say. "I am allowed out by myself sometimes.

"Oh, I just thought Maddy was coming too."

"Well, she isn't. I didn't ask her."

"Oh, well, come in then."

We go into the house, but I say, "Let's keep Lamb Chop company."

"Why? He's around somewhere."

"I thought he lived under the house. In that room."

"He was only in there because of the party. Normally he just roams around."

"Well, let's go down to your room, anyway."

"That's my private space."

"Yeah, I know," I say, "that's why I want to go down there. It will make getting to know you easier."

"Nobody but me normally goes down there."

"Well, if I'm meant to be your new sister, I think you'd better show me your den properly. Without Lamb Chop trying to eat me."

"It was Davy he didn't like."

"Yeah, well, whatever. Let's go and check the place out."

When we get to the downstairs room, Tristan unlocks it with a old fashioned key and we enter the gloom. The gloom is dimly lit by the computer screen, which is now infested with fish slowly swimming around and eating each other.

"Don't you ever turn that thing off?" I ask.

"It's bad for computers to be turned on and off all the time. It's much better to just let them run."

Tristan sits in the chair in front of the computer. He swivels it to face me. There is no other chair in the room, so I move a pile of books off the top of a big wooden box and sit on it. It's one of those huge wooden boxes with metal fittings at the corners and a fancy wrought iron lock.

"What do you keep in here?" I ask.

"Magic," Tristan says.

"Like hard boiled eggs?"

"That sort of thing," Tristan agrees, cagily.

"What else?" I ask.

"Severed limbs," Tristan says. "Bits of bodies."

"Yuk. Show me."

"Not now," Tristan says. "You'd freak. I'll show you some-time, though."

"Oh yeah."

We sit there in the semi-darkness for a couple of minutes. We don't say anything, but there's no strain. Then I say, "Are all these books yours?"

"They are now." Tristan gets up and starts flicking through

them. "Most of them used to belong to my grandfather. He was a famous psychoanalyst. I'm going to be one myself after I qualify in medicine."

"A shrink?" I say, incredulously. "You're going to be a shrink?"

"I wouldn't use that word. I find it rather silly. All the really great mysteries are in the mind. I often read Grandfather's old books. I've learnt lots from them. After I qualify as a doctor I'll have a head-start on the other trainee psychiatrists because of my reading."

"Most shrinks are madder than their patients," I tell him. "It's a well-known fact."

"That's just popular opinion. It's a defense mechanism. People don't like the idea that other people can see into their minds."

"Can you see into mine?"

"It would be unprofessional to tell you."

"Tell me what?"

"What is going on in your mind," Tristan says. He is getting quite agitated, but I feel I'm getting to see a side of him that he normally keeps hidden. He goes on, "You might not be able to handle the insight. Freud warned against *wild analysis*...that's when—"

"It's when some poor shrink's brain gets overheated and he starts making up stories. You're better off making up *real* stories. Proper novels and plays and poetry," I say. "I've been thinking of writing a science fiction story myself."

"What about?"

"Oh, telephones and all that. The past." I know it sounds a bit silly saying this, but probably not as silly as if I started to talk about Rod Gianforte straight out. I'd just be giving Tristan ammunition for his crazy psychiatric theories. Anyway, Tristan doesn't seem to think I'm silly.

"Tell me about this story," he says, all very calm and reasonable. Like a psychiatrist on telly, actually. Except that they usually turn out to have murdered their beautiful patients and taken to dressing up in their high heels.

"Well," I say, "in my story, the one I'm working on, I haven't actually written anything down yet, well, there's this guy who rings up from the past. Like there's this girl and the telephone rings and the caller is in another time."

"When? The Middle Ages? The Age of the Enlightenment?"

"Don't be a twit," I say. "They didn't have phones in those days."

"Well, maybe the caller could be talking into a magic conch shell or something like that and—"

"No. The caller is talking on a normal telephone. Only he's in 1960."

"That's too boring, Jenny. Hardly any time ago at all. Besides, my Dad says the early nineteen-sixties were very boring years. It didn't start to get controversial until about 1967. Why don't you put the caller on another planet and have—"

"Look, Tristan, this is *my* story. And the caller is in 1960. And he's in Sydney, okay?"

"All right. All right. I was only trying to be helpful."

"Yes. Well. Thanks. But Rod, this guy on the other end of the telephone, calls me up...calls up the girl in my story...and he tells her—"

I'm sitting in Tristan's bunker describing Rod and the telephone and he is listening in an interested sort of way. He doesn't make any more suggestions. I think he realizes that this is my story and I'm not looking for editorial help. It occurs to me as I'm talking to him that I'm beginning to like him a bit more. I mean, he *is* listening to me, which is a bit more than I could expect Davy or Mum or even Poppa to do.

When I finish my "story," Tristan asks, "How does it all end?"

"I don't know," I say. "We'll have to wait and see."

"*I'll* have to wait and see," Tristan says. "You can end it any way you want to."

"Yeah," I say without conviction, "I suppose I can."

There is a moment's silence. I decide to tell Tristan that it isn't really a "story," that it's real. Before I can speak, he says, "Anyway, tell me about Maddy."

"What's Maddy got to do with anything?"

"She's your best friend. So tell me about her. We're meant to be getting to know each other, so we'd better know about each other's friends."

He's right, of course. But at the moment I don't really want to talk about Maddy. Still, I suppose I ought to be polite, so I tell him a thing or two. I tell him about how Maddy isn't all that good at school work. I tell him that Maddy used to have a boyfriend called Jem, but he ditched her for an air-head called Bo which is short for Bimbo. Tristan listens intently, probably more intently than when he was listening to my story.

"Maddy's got beautiful eyes," he says.

I nearly die laughing. Tristan is annoyed.

"What's so funny?" he asks me.

"They're just ordinary old eyes, Tristan. You know: pupil, iris, cornea, cataract, eye lashes, focal point, contact lenses, bloodshot veins...."

"That's not funny, Jenny."

"Are you sure it's not her tits?" I say sarcastically. "I think what you *really* think is beautiful about Maddy is—"

I don't get to finish my sentence. Tristan leaps out of his chair and stands glowering at me. It looks like he is going to chuck a real mental. Even in the bad light of the bunker I can see that his face is all red.

"All right, Tristan," I say. "Only joking. Keep your wool on."

Slowly Tristan sits down again. The poor kid. He's in love with Maddy. Well, I suppose things could be worse, my new brother in love with my best friend.

After a bit more chat about nothing very important, I say I've got to go.

"I'll walk with you to the tram."

"That'd be good. Listen, why don't we all go skating next weekend?"

"Who, you and me and Davy?"

I wait a moment to tease him. "And Maddy."

Tristan shrugs. "Fine. Call me with the details."

When the tram comes, I'm half way up when I turn around. "I'll give your love to Maddy," I yell at Tristan, "You know, the one with the great tits...." But this time he doesn't blush.

"I know," Tristan yells from the curb.

The tram driver looks at me as if I'm a delinquent. He probably thinks I'm carrying a spray can. "No, it's true," I say to the tram driver, showing him my ticket. "My friend Maddy has perfect breasts."

"Just sit down, girlie," says the driver and starts the tram. I sit looking out of the window at all the nice houses and silly boutiques as they pass. When the tram finally rattles over the bridge, I look down on the muddy waters of the Yarra and suddenly think to myself that I'm completely happy. I'm probably happier than I've been at any time since Mum left home.

TRISTAN'S CASEBOOK:
April 29

The subject paid the present writer a visit. During the course of the interview she managed to contrive a fictional account of a series of telephone calls from someone in the past. It is obviously no accident that the caller from the past is represented as an older man. One feels that this man—to whom, no doubt significantly, she gave the name "Rod"—represents an idealized version of her inadequate father (who, we must remember, has proved himself wholly incapable of retaining the affections of his wife; the poor woman having been forced to seek the companionship of the present writer's own father). All attempts by the present writer to convince the subject that she should provide her "story" with a definitive ending failed. She became confused and evasive when asked to do so. The present writer interprets this inability to bring things to a proper conclusion as evidence of the subject's ambivalence in regard to her father.

The subject's relations with her girlfriend, the delightful Madeleine, are also a matter for some concern. When asked why she hadn't brought her friend with her, the subject became quite aggressive. That an enquiry as eminently reasonable as this one should produce such a reaction can only be seen as evidence of acute insecurity. Although the subject eventually relented slightly and talked about her friend Madeleine, it was only to make slighting remarks about her exam results. As she took her leave of the present writer, the subject went so far as to conjecture that the present writer's interest in the charming Madeleine—with whom an afternoon of skating is to be arranged—was the result of an infantile infatuation with certain parts of her anatomy. One can only think of the common phrase: "sour grapes."

SUNDAY, 30 APRIL, AFTERNOON

We stand around outside the Ice Arena waiting for Tristan. Maddy and I have been here before, but Davy has only ever used roller blades. He says he thinks ice skating is for English dorks in silly frocks. I think he's seen too much Torvil and Dean on the telly. He's being a bit silly if he thinks the scene inside the Ice Arena is going to be like that, but I don't say anything.

Davy mutters, "I hope Dweeb-Head doesn't try anything stupid. It would be a total bummer if we had to spend the afternoon carting him off to casualty."

I say, "Stop calling Tristan that."

Davy is surprised and offended. "You used to call him that yourself."

"Yeah, well I've changed."

"I don't know about you, Jenny."

"Oh do shut up, you two," Maddy says. "Here he comes now." and there's Tristan walking towards us with a tote bag swinging in his right hand. I wonder if he is going to give me a quick kiss like he did in the Time Zone Arcade. I half wish he would, just to get up Davy's nose. But he doesn't.

"Hello, Maddy," he says. "Nice to see you." It actually looks as if it's Maddy he wants to kiss, but doesn't quite dare to.

"Hello," says Maddy, suddenly all smiles. I feel a rush of jealousy, but don't want to admit it.

"Come on," Davy says. "We can't stand around all day."

We pay our money at the cash register and the girl says,

"Skate hire?"

"Yes," I say.

"Not for me," Tristan says and waves his tote bag merrily at the girl. The bag is quite heavy. He's got his own skates in it. The rest of us pay $1.50 extra and the girl gives us little plastic tokens.

While we are at the counter exchanging the tokens for skates Davy says, "Oh God, he's got little bed-socks for them." I glance across to where Tristan is sitting on a bench putting on his skates. His skates are brilliant black and gold. You can't see the blades because they've got these pink protective plastic covers. Tristan slips the covers off, and the blades are very bright stainless steel, as if they've never seen the ice.

"These should do youse," says the boy at the skate counter and dumps a pile of scuffed blue plastic hire skates in front of us. "If they don't fit, give us a yell and I'll get youse a new pair."

We sit on the bench next to Tristan and start taking off our shoes. Bad pop music is being played too loud, but it grinds to a halt and the DJ starts on about a cheerio to all the Kevins on the ice. A couple of girls further down the bench giggle. Tristan has just taken off the crappiest pair of old Dunlop Volleys I've ever seen. Both shoes have holes over the big toes and the laces are broken and tied together again. They are the color of dish-water. Davy sees them as well.

"Nice shoes," Davy says.

"You want to wear old shoes to the ice," Tristan says. "Then no one will steal them."

"I'd reckon," says Davy.

"We've hired a locker," says Maddy.

"It's all right," says Tristan, and pushes his crappy old shoes under the bench.

"No, really," says Maddy, "you can put your shoes in our locker."

"Phew!" says Davy.

"Oh do grow up," I snap.

In the end we all put our shoes in the locker, stuffing in

Tristan's tote bag and the pink blade-preservers as well, then stagger across the rubber matting to the ice. It's not too crowded. The air is as cold as a fridge, but then we *are in* a fridge. They have to keep the ice from melting. Natch. We all push off from the wooden retaining wall and glide across the ice.

To my surprise, we're not too bad at this. Davy wobbles a bit, but all that roller-blading has left him knowing what to do. We circle around the arena, at first together, then we start to get split up. The other skaters keep cutting across and getting between us. Besides, it's cool to just be on your own for a bit, whirling round, being blasted by the bad rock music.

Davy shoots past me. "Watch this, Jenny," he shouts and does a mad 180. Suddenly he's up in the air and twisting. Then he's gliding backwards. He teeters a bit, regains his balance and collides with this kid in a green bomber jacket. Neither of them falls over.

"Watch it, mate," says the kid.

"Sorry, mate," says Davy.

Then Tristan starts performing, and he's shockingly good. He skates backwards like Davy—but he does it on one leg, sticking the other leg out horizontally behind him. Or perhaps it's *in front* of him, considering that he is going backwards. Tristan doesn't wobble one little bit. He sails round in a graceful curve and suddenly spins to face forwards again. He zooms away.

"Try-hards," Maddy says, suddenly appearing beside me, "the pair of them." But she sounds secretly impressed to me.

Then Davy and Tristan are racing each other. Tristan is faster, so Davy does a method. Something I've seen him do on roller blades: jumping into the air and catching hold of the skates with his hands. I've only ever seen him do it by jumping off something, like steps or a low concrete wall. But the ice is all flat, there's nothing to jump off. He doesn't get very far into the air and crashes down in a heap. Tristan circles round and offers Davy a hand up. Davy says something I can't catch, but it sounds aggressive to me. He pushes Tristan's hand away and gets to his feet. He shoots off and I lose sight of him.

Minutes later Maddy and I are fooling about trying to skate in unison with our arms round each other's waists. Tristan and Davy flash past. They are deliberately trying to bump one another.

"Heav-vy...," Maddy says.

Next time the boys pass us they are going at top speed. Davy bumps Tristan. Tristan wobbles, regains his balance and manages to get in front of Davy. They collide. Tristan is down on the ice.

Davy's skate goes straight over Tristan's hand, cutting one of his fingers off.

Tristan screams and clutches his maimed hand to his stomach. The severed finger lies on the ice in a small splotch of blood.

I can't believe it. I can't believe what I've just seen. Davy is unaware of what he has done. He keeps skating, disappears into the crowd. But other people have seen what happened. There is a shocked group of skaters around Tristan. His finger lies on the ice—horrible to look at. The severed end is all bloody, with a bit of white bone showing through the red tattered flesh.

Tristan lies on the ice, eyes tightly shut. His injured hand is still held tightly to his stomach. Someone asks him if he is all right. It's the most ridiculous question I've ever heard. A couple of the younger skaters are sobbing and gasping. One little kid is as white as a ghost. Another one looks like he is going to throw up.

Beside me Maddy starts to giggle. She gets completely hysterical.

"Shut up, Maddy," I tell her, aghast. But it's no good. She keeps giggling. Tears are running down her face, ruining her eye makeup. I leave her and go over to Tristan. His face is contorted in pain. I kneel down beside him and put a tentative hand on his shoulder. Before I can say anything to him, he jack-knifes into a sitting position, scrambles to his feet and swoops on his severed finger. Still holding his injured hand to his stomach, he hurtles off after Davy, waving the severed finger in the air with his other hand.

"You bastard!" I hear him yell. "You cut my best finger off."

I think I'm going to be sick. I get to my feet. Maddy is hopelessly hysterical, she's laughing like a drain. I might have to slap her face. That's what you do with hysterical people—it jolts them back to reality. But I just say, "Please shut up, Maddy."

Maddy says through the laughter, "That's better than an egg." She's obviously unhinged. She's making no sense at all.

"Maddy, I'll have to slap your face."

"Oh Gawd," says Maddy. "You believe it! Oh, Jenny, Jenny, you think it's real." She's almost convulsed with laughter.

I look wildly around. The expressions on the faces of the other skaters are a mixture of shock and bewilderment. But some of them are starting to grin. They think it's a joke. Maddy thinks it's a joke. Davy and Tristan come screaming past. Tristan is still holding one hand to his stomach and waving the severed finger around with the other. "You'll pay for this...," he yells.

There's a blur as a big guy, *Ice Arena—Staff* embroidered on his jacket, takes off in pursuit of Davy and Tristan. It doesn't take him very long to catch the pair of them. He shoves them both towards the exit, holding onto their collars. Tristan takes his hand away from his stomach. There's nothing wrong with his hand: all five fingers are alive and wriggling. Tristan puts the severed finger into his pocket. Just outside the exit, standing on the rubber matting, is a red-haired guy in a suit. He must be the manager, and he doesn't look pleased. I'm not pleased myself. Maddy seems to think life is a total hoot.

"You buy them in joke shops," she says to me. "You know, you can get hideous wounds and fake puke and rubber dog poop."

"It's not funny, Maddy," I snap at her, "I thought it was real."

I look to where the guy in the suit is heavying the two boys. I can't hear what he is saying, but the boys are standing looking down at their skates. The man demands something. Tristan puts his hand in his pocket and produces the severed finger. The man in the suit stands there, contemptuously turning the thing over in his hand. He turns and walks away, taking the finger with him. Davy and Tristan make their way back onto the ice. They look pretty low. Slowly they skate over to Maddy and me.

Davy says to Tristan, "There was no need to call that sleezebag 'Sir' all the time."

"Well, you didn't call him anything. You didn't say anything at all."

"It wasn't my finger," Davy says.

"Wasn't mine either. Look." Tristan displays his hands, wriggling all ten fingers. "You must have cut someone else's finger off. You want to look where you're going."

"I'll bet you don't dare go and get that rubber finger back when we leave," Davy says. "You won't have the guts to go along to the manager's office and say, 'Please Sir, I'm leaving, Sir, can I have my finger back, Sir.' That guy'll take your finger home with him and play tricks on his kids."

"What about your ear?" Tristan says.

"What *about* my ear?"

Tristan reaches across and pulls something out of Davy's ear. This time it's not an egg. It's another ear—all covered in blood.

Davy slaps his hand up to his ear. And looks foolish for a second. Then he pushes Tristan hard in the chest. "You bum," he says, "you've cut off my best ear." Tristan skates away. Davy zooms off after him. "Give me back my ear," he yells. I see the bouncer in the *Staff* jacket eyeing the boys coldly.

"Let's pretend we don't know them," I say to Maddy.

"Lighten up, Jenny," Maddy says. "It's like that painter, what's-his-name."

"Van Gogh," I tell her.

"Yeah, him," Maddy says. "He cut off his ear for love. He sent it to his one true love. I saw this video. Maybe the boys love us."

"Help," I say and start skating. Maddy comes up beside me and soon we are skating in unison again, our arms round each others' waists. Maddy, I can feel, is starting to giggle again. Suddenly I am too. "Greater love hath no boy," I say, "than he pull a plastic ear off another boy's face."

"See," Maddy says. "You have got a sense of humor, Jenny. You're just a bit slow."

§

We end up eating hamburgers in a fast food outlet. At least the others are all eating hamburgers. I don't feel like one myself, so I just eat fries out of Davy's paper bucket. It's funny how boys make friends. Tristan and Davy are now the best of mates—all because they both copped an earful from the Ice Arena manager. They fool about, getting more stupid by the minute.

"What about a whole leg?" Davy proposes. "Just lying there on the ice. Cut off at the knee. Or the hip." In a deep and gravelly voice, like a horror movie, he moans: "*The Severed Leg.*"

"It's no joke, you can buy them," Tristan says. "They use them for training ambulance crews. Totally lifelike. But they'd be expensive."

"We could make one," suggests Davy, really getting into it. "We could get some raw meat. You know, a leg of beef or something...."

"And we could dress it up in an old track-suit. With, say, an old skate at one end and then all the meat sticking out of the torn-off top bit."

"We'd need a lot of blood...."

"Easy. Tomato sauce."

"Speaking of which," says Davy, reaching for the ketchup bottle, "have you got any more fingers?"

"Sure," says Tristan, "What do you want? Little finger? Thumb? Finger with wedding ring?"

"Just an ordinary finger," Davy says.

Tristan leans down and rummages in his tote bag. He produces a new plastic finger in its own little pool of plastic blood and passes it over. Davy takes the top bun off his half-eaten hamburger and arranges the severed finger on the meat. It really is a sickening sight. To complete the effect, he picks up the plastic ketchup container, shaped like a red tomato, and squeezes a bit more "blood" onto the finger.

"Gross-out!" shrieks Maddy, like it's the wildest thing she's ever seen.

Davy takes the hamburger over to the counter. The boy behind the counter is wearing a red baseball cap with the fast food outlet's logo on its brim. He can't be much older than me. Fifteen maybe.

"Hey, mate," Davy says. "I think you ought to check the kitchen staff. There's been a bit of an accident."

The kid glances without much interest at the half-eaten hamburger. Then does a double-take. It looks as if he is going to spew straight over the counter. From out in the kitchen, somehow making the whole scene much worse, there's the sudden hiss of somebody squashing more hamburger meat onto the hot plate. Two girls standing by the counter, waiting to order, peer over at where Davy is waving the hamburger about.

"Aw, yuckoh," says one girl.

The other girl goes green, and her cheeks bulge, but she doesn't say anything.

"How much of it did you *eat*?" says the first girl.

"Most of it," says Davy.

The kid in the baseball hat lurches away from the counter and staggers out into the kitchen. The talkative girl says, "What did it taste like?"

"Real tasty," says Davy. "I think I'll have the rest." He picks the finger off the hamburger and pops it into his mouth. The green girl goes even greener. Her friend lets out a hoot of laughter.

"Far out!" she yells.

Across the table from me, Maddy falls in a giggling heap. Her giggles turn to chokes and gurgles as the hamburger she's eating goes down the wrong way. Tristan starts to thump her on the back with one hand while putting his other arm right round her.

"Maddy, darling," Tristan says, "Don't leave me now. You are too young and fair of face to die!"

He collapses all over Maddy, convulsed by his own wit. Maddy is choking and laughing at the same time. A bit of half-eaten hamburger flies out of her mouth and hits the green-faced girl on the bare leg. The girl squeals and jumps back in horror.

Maddy and Tristan are a gibbering heap. It's the most disgusting scene I've ever witnessed. Over by the counter Davy is standing with his mouth closed over the plastic finger, looking like a goldfish that's swallowed a cat. The kid in the baseball cap comes out of the kitchen accompanied by a big guy of about thirty wearing a dirty apron over a pair of football shorts. His blue singlet leaves his arms bare. His arms are long and hairy and covered in ferocious tats. He takes one look at Davy. He takes one look at Tristan and Maddy. I try to look as if I don't know these people. The big guy raises one arm and points with the greasy stainless steel spatula he's holding. First he points at Davy. Then he points at our table. Davy spits the finger into his hand and holds it up like a trophy.

"You arseholes," the cook says quietly. "Out! Now!"

He points the spatula at the door, and it's obvious that he's very, very angry. Next thing I know I'm halfway out of the door with Maddy. Close behind us surge Tristan and Davy. The last sound I hear before we are all reach the cool night air of the street is the green-faced girl puking like a fire hydrant. We set off down the street at an extremely rapid pace—just in case the guy with the spatula decides to follow us.

"Where do we go now?" Davy says. I get the idea he wants to go some place where he can repeat his trick.

"Madeleine and I are thinking of going to the pictures," says Tristan.

"We are?" says Maddy.

"Aren't we?" asks Tristan.

Maddy giggles and says, "Sure we are."

I say, "I'm going home."

"Jeez, Jen." Davy pulls a face. "You don't have to be home for hours. Let's go to the movies with Mad and Tristan."

"I don't feel like the movies," I tell them. "I feel like going home. You can come too if you like."

"Aw, all right, Jenny." Davy says, "We can watch a video."

"I was thinking of doing my homework. I'll help you with yours too, if you'd like me to."

"Hey, really?" says Davy. He's always trying to get people to help him with his homework. Usually it's me.

"Well, we'll see you party-poopers later," says Maddy. "Come on, Tris."

§

Davy and I walk over to the nearest tram stop. I lean against the safety rail. In the distance I can see Maddy and Tristan walking towards the Cinema Complex. They have their arms around each other's waists.

"Tristan's not a bad guy," Davy says. "For a dweeb."

TRISTAN'S CASEBOOK:
April 30

The present writer had an interesting and informative time at an ice skating rink and fast food outlet yesterday. The subject and her lumpen friend were accompanied by their charming companion, Madeleine. After some high jinks on the ice, during which the present writer amused the crowd with witty severed-digit jests, the jolly foursome retired to Harry's Hamburger Heaven where further escapades took place. The lumpen young man showed a surprising ability at employing the severed-digit joke in the novel guise of a hamburger insert. The delightful Madeleine showed her appreciation of these larks in free-spirited and uninhibited merriment. Alas, the same cannot be said for the subject who remained tight-lipped and disapproving throughout. The present writer must confess to feeling a little relieved when the subject took her lumpen friend away to attend to their studies. This left the beautiful Madeleine free to give her undivided attention to the present writer during the viewing of *Rogue Cop III* at the Cinema Complex. A most pleasant interlude followed the viewing of the film. Madeleine, oh Madeleine, Maddy. Mad mad Madeleine your kisses are sweeter than wine.

The present writer here records and acknowledges his growing infatuation with the subject's friend, Ms. Madeleine Smith.

TUESDAY, 2 MAY, AFTERNOON

Everyone is packing up after physics and I'm keen to get out of the place and go home. It's been a long day. Mrs. Levine comes over to me as everyone's crashing and banging their way out of the room. "Jenny, could we have a little chat?"

"Huh? Sure."

We wander over to her desk and she goes on for a while about resolving vectors, which I know all about anyway. It seems to me that she's just waffling, waiting for everyone else to leave the room. I'm not sure I want this little "chat." A couple of kids are still mucking about with Bunsen burners and Mrs. Levine says to them, "Leave that stuff. I'll put it away later."

This is the first time in my life I've heard a teacher say she'll tidy up after her students. The other kids are pretty amazed as well. They look at each other and shrug and grab their school bags and leave the room. So there's just me and Mrs. Levine. She clears her throat and says, "How is your story coming along?"

Huh? Oh—she means that science fiction "story" I told her I was writing about getting a phone call from the past. When I'd told her, she'd got it all wrong—she'd thought my "story" was really about Mum leaving us and going to live with Edward. I decide I don't want to have any more of this sort of discussion. So I say, "Oh, I've given that up. I'm not writing it any more. All that stuff about changing the past is too difficult."

Mrs. Levine says, "Yes, I think we have to accept that there is nothing we can do about things that have already happened.

We just have to work at making the present as satisfactory as possible and plan for the best conceivable future."

Poor woman, she's still on about my home life. I start to bring the interview to a close by telling her that absolutely everything is wonderful at home, when she says, "You've been doing really well at school, Jenny. At least in science."

"Yeah, I know," I say, "I'm crash-hot at science." This is true: I'm extremely good at physics and chemistry. I'm a legend. Mrs. Levine looks just a little taken aback. I think she thinks a bit of false modesty might be appropriate. Then she seems to get a grip on herself—she's meant to be encouraging girls to do science, to have a strong self-image of themselves as scientists. And here I am: Ms. Positive Self-Image herself. So Mrs. Levine says, "Well, I'm glad you are so confident, Jenny."

"Come the final exams, I think I'll top the State."

"Well, you never know, but...."

Suddenly I'm starting to enjoy this little "chat." So I say, "That'll stick it up the Vietnamese."

"Jenny!" Mrs. Levine, shocked, is on firmer ground here. She's not meant to be encouraging ethnic conflict. "I wouldn't have expected that sort of remark from you, of all people!"

Actually the poor thing does look pretty staggered. But to keep the gag going, I say, "Well, they can't be the only ones getting perfect scores *every* year."

"Jenny, while it is true that many of the top students are Vietnamese, it is also true that they work very hard indeed. If you had come to Australia on a leaky boat...."

"No, Mrs. Levine," I say earnestly, "it's got nothing to do with leaky old boats. It's because they are *more intelligent than us.* The Vietnamese have got more brains. Well, more brains than *most* of us. But me, Mrs. Levine, I'm different. I'm a legend. I work very hard too, and I'm as bright as a Vietnamese."

Mrs. Levine can't think of anything to say. I start giggling then, which gives it away. And Mrs. Levine suddenly catches on.

"Jenny!" she says crossly, but she's relieved all the same. "I take it that you are being satirical? I take it that you are sending up what you see as stuffy, middle-class liberal values?"

"Could be," I say, looking at the floor.

"Well, just be careful, my girl. It is very easy to be misunderstood."

"Like you misunderstood my story about telephones working across time," I say.

"How did I misunderstand that?" Mrs. Levine asks, puzzled.

"You thought it was about my home situation. About Mum moving out and getting engaged to that creep."

"Oh, and it isn't?"

"No. It's about what I said it was about: someone in the past ringing up someone in the present."

"Well, it's your story, Jenny. So I suppose you know what it is about." Mrs. Levine looks almost embarrassed. I can tell that she isn't too keen to abandon her theory about my "story." She adds, "But...er.... Anyway, Jenny. Do you mind if I talk to you personally for a minute?"

This is truly weird. The poor thing must be going off her rocker. First she tells a couple of students she'll put their equipment away, then she *asks* me if I mind if she talks to me— personally. Who ever heard of a teacher asking for permission to talk to you? I'm starting to get worried. I'm also a bit intrigued: I want to know what she's on about.

"Yeah, sure, Mrs. Levine. Feel free to speak."

"Jenny. You used to be so neat," she says and then stops.

"Uh, *neat*?" She must be talking about my handwriting. "You can still read my homework, can't you?" I say. "Anyway, I print most of it on the computer. Just because I don't write like a primary school kid anymore...."

"No," Mrs. Levine says, cutting in, "I don't mean your handwriting—although that could do with a bit more care and attention. There was a time, Jenny, when you would never have worn jeans like that to school."

She's looking down at my jeans, which do have these ragged cuffs. We're allowed to wear jeans to school, only they have to be "school jeans." The authorities can't get away from the idea that it's their job to make you wear a uniform, but they know they have to be "responsive to the needs and aspirations of today's youth"—so they try to turn proper clothes, like jeans, into a sort of uniform. Except that the type of proper clothes they decide you are allowed to wear are all up the nerd end of the spectrum. The whole thing sucks. When I'd bought the jeans, they had been too long. I was going to take them up properly with the sewing machine. But then I thought, screw it, and I just cut them down to size with a pair of scissors. Now they've got these wicked gross-out cuffs: all frayed.

"That's deliberate, Mrs. Levine. I like them like this."

"Oh, I'm sure you do, Jenny. Tell me, why didn't you iron your shirt?"

I wouldn't have expected this. I really wouldn't have expected anybody as cool as Mrs. Levine to start cracking on about my clothes. I'm about to go into a major fit of quiet sulks but I remember that she asked me if she could speak personally and I've gone and given her permission. So I tell her, "Look, I didn't think it was going to get so hot today. So I ironed the collar and I ironed the cuffs. See, I thought I was going to wear my sweater all day. There's no point in wearing ironed clothes *under* other clothes. And anyway," I go on, "I'm not the only one. There were a couple of teachers I noticed at lunchtime looking just like me: nice smooth collar and cuffs, all scrumpled in the middle. Look at Mr. Ironside!"

"Some of my colleagues, I admit, are a bit untidy."

"Some of your colleagues, Mrs. Levine, are total bums."

"Jenny! I really can't tolerate—"

"You said you wanted to talk *personally*. It was you who started on about *my* clothes."

For a moment Mrs. Levine is silent. I look at her, sitting behind her desk. She really is very pretty. She's my favorite teacher by miles, except that I can't understand why she calls herself "Mrs. Levine" instead of "Dr. Levine', unless it's to save the Principal the embarrassment of not having that sort of qualification. I'm also beginning to think I must be her favorite student. She's wearing this real cool gray silk shirt with a rose embroidered on the tip of one collar. The shirt shows off her boobs nicely. The shirt is very well ironed. She's got a silver chain round her neck. It might have a locket or a cross or something at the lowest point. But the lowest point is hidden by the gray silk. She smiles at me and says, "Look, Jenny, all I really wanted to say was that you can be a good scientist and look neat and tidy at the same time."

"Albert Einstein didn't seem to think so. He didn't even wear socks."

Mrs. Levine laughs.

"That's very good, Jenny. But there's no real need to look like Einstein. It's just that the clothes we wear often reflect our inner selves. You've been looking so...er...dowdy lately that I can't help wondering—"

Mrs. Levine doesn't finish the sentence, but I know what she means: she's worried about me. And maybe I am her favorite student. So I just say, "Not to worry, Mrs. Levine, I'm not going to get an ear-ring through my eyelid."

She shudders. "I hope not. I can't imagine anything more... er...*uncomfortable*."

"Neither can I," I say as I grab my bag and hit the track. "We agree on the really important issues. See you."

"Good afternoon, Jenny," Mrs. Levine says with a slightly sad note in her voice as I zip out the door. Teachers are weird.

SATURDAY, 6 MAY, AFTERNOON

Tristan phones me after the Science Show and suggests that we go for a bike ride together.

"It's too far for me to ride to Kew," I tell him.

"No, I'll come over to your place by tram."

"How can you take a bike on the tram?"

Tristan laughs. "You great dill, don't you remember? Your mother said I could borrow hers. How about you get it out of the shed and pump up the tires for me, and I'll whiz over right now. We could go down along the Merri creek bike path."

"Won't you be embarrassed, riding a girl's bike?"

"It's a trail bike, your mum said. Who would know the difference?" He sounds a bit exasperated. "Anyway, that's a pretty sexist remark, coming from you. I mean, what's the difference?"

I feel quite nettled by this, because it's a sensitive spot of mine. Usually I'm the one to complain about people making distinctions based on sex and gender when they're irrelevant. "Well, some boys wouldn't, that's all. Some boys are afraid of being laughed at."

He grunts. "Davy might be, I suppose. Surely you've noticed by now that I don't worry what people think of me."

That's true, but I try to wiggle out of it. "I bet you'd feel pretty stupid if you had to wear a dress! Or, I dunno, a pink woolen cardigan."

"You can keep your cardigan," Tristan says. "But I've worn a kilt, and that's like a dress. Anyway, didn't you ever see the clothes Greek soldiers wear when they're feeling sentimental? Little frilly skirts and pom-poms on their boots."

I burst out laughing. He's right—it's in an Encarta history file. Weird. "Okay, come on over. Poppa's at the university, but he'll be back for tea—I'll have to be home by six. Anyway, I don't think we've got any batteries for Mum's bike lights."

Tris is wearing perfectly ordinary clothes when he rings the door bell, which is a relief. I've hauled Mum's old trail bike in from the back yard and cleaned it a bit, plus pumped up its fat tires. Tristan throws one leg over the seat and jigs up and down for a moment.

"Hey, this is just the right height. Thought I might have to adjust it." He digs out a small tool kit from his tote bag, which he's thrown in the wire basket mounted over the back wheel, and waves it at me.

"Always prepared for everything, aren't you, Tristan? You must have been a boy scout."

"Not me," he says disdainfully. "Carlos either. We left that kind of macho nonsense to our big brother Alain."

"Come on." I slam the door behind us. The sun is out and the day is autumny but nice. The air is lovely. "Let's go. There's this place I want to show you."

Rathdowne Street is too busy for good cycling, so I lead Tris down to Canning Street, which also has a green median strip but much less traffic. We pedal without saying much up to Park Street, at the boundary with Brunswick, which is a much poorer suburb. Park turns one-way after a bit, but there's a cute pathway that you can use to get almost all the way to Rushall railway station, which is perched high over the Merri Creek. We're puffing a bit by the time we go down through the creepy underpass beneath the station, and I'm glad Tristan is with me because I always have a little fear that some horrible man will jump out of the shadows and grab me. There's no one there, luckily, except a tiny foreign lady from the old folks' home next to the railway, and she waves happily to us as we get off our bikes and push up the slope to the narrow bridge leading from

Carlton to yet another suburb, Northcote. All the suburbs come together at this one point. It's a hub, this place. Four suburbs stretching away in four different directions. Here you can go from one to the other in a few steps. Maybe time works the same way. All you need to do is find the hub and you can step from one time zone to another. Hell, they tell us space and time can't really be separated.

"Space zones," I mutter. "Spacetime zones."

"What?"

"Oh, nothing. It's just, this place reminds me of me and Rod, this guy who—" I stop. The sun doesn't reach the water flowing below us in a deep cutting. "Well, it's in my science fiction story."

Tristan gazes into my eyes like a doctor with a wild new theory. "Wow, you're really obsessing about this story, Jenny. I sometimes get the feeling that you think it's real."

I hesitate for a long moment. I'd love to tell him that it *is* real, and that it's about to change history, but he'd just think I'm crazy. "Sometimes it feels real," I say. "I've been thinking about it for days. Anyway, it's about these two people in different time zones, this girl now and this old guy in the past. Well, he's not *that* old, but he is by now." I stop in confusion. "If you see what I mean."

Tristan, to my surprise, is looking rather impressed. "You really are a very interesting person, Jenny Kane. I'm glad we've become friends. I'm even glad we're going to become brother and sister." He grins and looks away shyly. "It's a pity we didn't bring Maddy with us, though."

"Oh, you're the one who's obsessed!" I push him on the shoulder, and get back on my bike. "Come on, let's go across the bridge as fast as we can. It's a real buzz!"

The narrow bridge dips slightly in the middle, and it rattles like a thousand old bones. Down below, vegetation is green and brown, and the water gurgles through rock. My bike's wheels thump and bump.

"Hey, that was great." Tristan jumps off when we reach the

far side, and returns to peer into the creek bed. "I love bridges. How did you know?" Beneath his borrowed safety helmet, his face is flushed.

"I didn't. But if you like bridges, you'll love the place we're going next."

You have to zig and zag along the side of the Merri creek before you get to the main street, and eventually there's this big steel bridge that carries the railway lines across the Merri. A Reservoir train rumbles overhead, tremendously noisy, as if the whole world is shaking, as we get off and lock our bikes together to a NO PARKING sign with my fabulous new bike lock. The bridge that spans the Merri is edged by waste land full of bushes and broken stone and rusting old car bodies. I know it's probably even more dangerous than going under the Rushall station underpass, but it's great—a place that's right in the middle of town and yet it looks like a piece of the country, or Mad Max territory, or something.

"You want us to go down there?" Tristan asks. "Doesn't look very interesting. Anyway, there could be snakes, you know."

"There are," I tell him. "There's warning signs. I've never seen one, though." I point to the rock wall of the railway bridge. "Look up there."

"Oh." Tristan's eyes gleam. "Fabulous! A pedestrian walkway!"

"Come on, I'll race you to the middle."

We run up the steps and then belt along this really narrow metal pathway that's hanging suspended under one side of the rails. The barrier to our right is just metal and wire, you can see right through it, and when you run it seems to disappear. It's as if you're running in the sky. The sound is really strange, banging and echoing. We stop halfway across, right over the creek far below. Tristan sucks at his mouth and builds up a huge spitball and lets fly straight down, but the breeze grabs his little drop of gleaming spit and carries it away to the rocks.

"You must be a genius, Jenny," he says. His glasses catch the light of the afternoon sun. "This is exactly what I love."

"Of course I'm a genius," I say modestly, leaning back to stare up at the train tracks. "The really terrific thing is when a train goes over. There should be one any minute—"

I hear, then, *from up above me*, "Fantastic!" and my blood sort of runs cold. I turn around, and start to scream Tristan's name, and stop myself in the nick of time because I don't want to scare him or throw him off balance, because the bloody idiot has climbed up on to the handrail of the pedestrian walkway and is standing in the sky, one foot behind the other, arms outstretched like a circus acrobat.

He takes one step, foot out into space, then back in front. And another step.

My heart literally stops.

It starts again, with a bang surely loud enough to scare Tristan off his perch. But in fact I'm the only one who hears it. Tristan is singing! Tristan is cavorting along in the pale light, swaying slightly, twenty or forty meters above a cold brown creek and smashed rocks and hard tree branches, and the idiot is humming and crooning to himself like a happy child with a brand new Christmas present!

"Tristan!" I try to say, but nothing comes out. My throat is totally dry. For the first time in my life, I'm actually, literally terrified. I haven't got a clue what to say to get him down. Out of my mouth come words that seem to appear from nowhere:

"I'm starving."

Tristan looks down at me, over his shoulder, and sways slightly. I go rigid with terror.

"Me too," he says amiably, and reaches into his shirt pocket. "Luckily, I have a Mars Bar." He pulls it out, tears the foil open with his teeth.

"Tristan, please come down," I wheeze in a tiny voice.

"Can't hear you, why don't you hop up here with me, the view's terrific."

At first I think it's my heart pounding like a machine in my chest, but it's not, it's an electric train rumbling toward us around the curve of the track from the northern stations, thumping and thundering toward the bridge. I press myself back against a steel stanchion and try not to scream. Tristan swivels on one foot and spins in midair, standing now on the aerobic heels of his hightops with his back to the endless fall behind him, staring up toward the approaching train. Its yellow headlights reflect from his glasses. I wonder if I'll have the slightest chance of rushing forward with my hand outstretched when he slips and tumbles into the gulf.

"I'm glad you've got a Mars Bar," I squawk. "But what about me? I said I was hungry first."

"You can have it," Tristan yells through the roar of the train. Lights from its windows flash and shadow, flash and shadow as it crashes above us. Everything shakes. "I've got a little treat of my own." Tristan reaches into his ear, pulls out an egg, crouches down on his haunches, whacks the egg on the vibrating handrail under his feet, breaks it open, scattering shell everywhere, pops the cold boiled egg into his mouth, and tosses the Mars Bar to me. I put out my numb hand. Too late. The confection sails through my grasp, hits the metal grid under my equally numb feet, bounces once, sails through a wire gap into the open sky. Horrified, I watch its dark chocolate tumble away in the vague light.

I can't stand up any longer. My legs give way, and I subside on to the cold metal surface. It's painted white, but the paint is crackled from the weather. Tristan, whose right cheek is bulging with boiled egg, looks at me with stricken eyes. He chews hard, once, twice, and swallows the egg. Then he jumps down lightly on to the pedestrian bridge, and grabs my hand.

"Jenny, are you all right?"

Angrily, I shake him off. "You bloody idiot!"

"Look, I'm sorry, okay?"

"You could have been killed." There are tears in my eyes. "Come on, we've got to get back, it's getting late, Poppa will be furious."

"It's not that late," Tris says sulkily. "Anyway, it wasn't dangerous, I've been doing it for years." He tries to grin at me, and it's not very convincing. "You should have seen your face!"

I stomp back along the bridge and down the metal stairs at the end and unlock the bikes and push mine on to the street, flicking on the headlight and the blinking red tail light. "You scared me, you stupid thing."

"Jenny." When I look around, he's just standing there, looking downcast, hands in his pockets. His voice is dejected. "Hang on a bit. I want to explain."

"You don't have to explain it to me, I'm just the cowardly girl you just got a thrill out of by scaring her half out of her mind." But I wait, holding the handlebars, until he lifts his eyes and meets my gaze.

"You're not cowardly, Jenny," he says, "and you're not half out of your mind. I was, though, a few years ago." He stops, and I can see him screwing up his courage, so I give him a little smile of encouragement. It's hard to stay angry at Tristan.

"What, literally out of your mind?"

"That's right. Literally. I'm still seeing a shrink, you know."

"A psychiatrist?"

"A Freudian psychoanalyst, actually. Twice a week."

I stare at him. "Is that why you're so interested in all that mental stuff? In your diary."

Tristan gives me a very suspicious look, then shrugs. "My CASEBOOK. Partly. As I said the other day, it's part of my family background—but yeah, I suppose it's transference."

"What's that?"

"Never mind." He pushes his bike into the grass to let a young yuppie couple jog past with their German Pointers, and then props it on its fold-down leg. He digs into his tote bag and pulls out another Mars Bar. "Go you halves."

"Okay." I prop my own bike, and we sit down on a patch of short grass. Another train clanks past overhead, this one coming home from the city. People are silhouetted in the windows, staring out into the early twilight, reading newspapers, talking or just sitting.

"I sort of went mad for a couple of years after my mother

killed herself," Tristan tells me.

My skin goes cold all over. Suicide! This really is freaky. It's nothing like having your mum go and live with someone else. I mean: I've *still got* Mum, even if I don't live with her. Tristan's mother has left him forever.

"Sorry," I stammer, "I didn't know."

"That's all right," Tristan says. "I'm over it now. Well, sort of."

"Look, if you go fooling around on bridges like that, you can't be all that...er...."

"Sane?"

"Well, er," I say, searching for the right word, "you know, *stable*."

"Oh, I'm very stable, Jenny. You saw me, I didn't fall off."

"I don't mean that sort of *stable*."

"Oh, I see, you mean *stable*!" Very seriously, like a worried teacher, Tristan says, "I'm not a horse, Jenny."

"I don't mean...," I start to say, but Tristan suddenly packs up. "You bum!" I yell at him, "you just love playing word games, don't you? You knew what I meant."

And then both of us are lying next to our bikes on the grass and all the discarded cigarette packets and the dried lumps of dog poop, convulsed. It seems to be the funniest thing either of us has ever heard. We're lying there laughing and crying and spluttering words like *horse* and *stable* and *cracked* and *oats*. I know that these words really aren't all that funny—but it's just the relief. After being scared out of my wits and then learning that Tristan's Mum committed suicide, it's good to able to laugh at something ridiculous.

"Look, we'd better go home," I say at last. "You can tell me about this psychoanalyst on the way."

We get back on our bikes and start home. The sun's definitely getting low and red in the sky, and the wind is rather cold. Tristan is silent for a while and then he says, "After Mum died, I went quite loopy. I sort of, you know, crawled away inside myself. I didn't want to know about the outside world. I didn't like it. I'm still a bit like that. That's why I go and see Dr. Grogan twice a week."

I'm not sure if I should say anything, so I don't. Tristan goes on, "When Mum died I started having all these fantasies. I'd make up stories about myself. And I'd believe them."

"We all do that," I say with a shrug that makes my bike bell tingle. "Everybody makes up stories about themselves."

"Yeah, but I really believed mine," Tristan says. "I didn't know where my mind stopped and the real world began. In my mind I was a super-hero, I could do anything. Fly, almost. I nearly tried it a couple of times."

"Flying?"

"Yeah, like off a building or a high cliff."

"But you didn't?" I say.

He shoots me a sarcastic glance. "Well, no, as you see I'm still in one piece."

I can be just as sarcastic back. "No, you just dance around on bridges."

"Yeah," Tristan says, "that was a bit silly wasn't it?"

"It was bloody madness."

"See, it's just that sometimes I feel completely invincible. Nothing can happen to me. I am in total control. If I say I won't fall off the bridge, then I won't."

"One day you might," I say.

"I hope not. Part of me knows that doing things like that is just dumbo, real stupid, destructive. But when I'm doing it, I'm such a super-hero that the other part of me takes over completely."

We pedal along the bike path in silence for a while. Then Tristan says, "I'm like that about people as well."

"What do you mean?" I say, "*about people...?*"

"I feel superior to everyone. I can see inside their minds. I can look down from a great height and watch everybody scurrying around like ants. They think they're free and independent—but really I understand them better than they understand themselves. They've got no free will."

"Is that what your *CASEBOOK* is all about?" I ask.

Tristan goes ballistic this time. "Look, how did you find out about my *CASEBOOK*?" he yells.

"Take it easy, Tristan," I say. "You'll fall off your bike."

"No one's meant to know about my *CASEBOOK*, it's mine. It's private."

"Maybe *you're* the ant," I suggest, feeling rather clumsy and nervous but not wanting to admit it, "and I'm looking down from a great height on *you* and seeing everything that goes on in *your* mind."

But Tristan is right off his rocker. I'm really sorry now that I teased him like that, but it's too late for regrets.

"You can't!" he shouts like a loon. "You're lying, Jenny! Nobody sees inside my mind. Even Dr. Grogan can't see inside my mind. She only knows what I *choose* to tell her."

"It's all right, Tristan," I say, getting off and pushing my bike up on to the Rathdowne St footpath. "Take a chill pill. I don't really know what's in your *CASEBOOK*. I just saw a little bit of it. Remember? When Davy and me were being monstered by your dog. I shouldn't have done it, but I did. Sorry."

We've arrived outside our front door. Without saying anything we push our bikes into the hallway. It will be terrible if Tristan goes home still angry with me, so I force myself to say, "Come in the kitchen, why don't you eat with us? Poppa won't be home for another half hour, but I've got to start cooking."

For a moment it looks as if Tristan is going to refuse my offer. He's never met Poppa, but he has to, sometime. Instead of refusing, to my surprise, he takes off his jacket and says, "Sure, why not?" We go into the kitchen and I organize him into making chocolate thickshakes in the blender while I peel some spuds. When he's finished flailing the thickshake mixture to an aerated sludge, he says, "Anyway, I'm not really very proud of what I write in my *CASEBOOK*. I don't treat people very nicely. I've written some stuff about you, Jenny. It's sort of true, but it's all, you know, *cold*."

"So why do you write it?" I ask.

"Sometimes, when I'm feeling angry or insecure or something, then it makes me feel better. But it's just fantasy. It's just a way of making myself feel powerful. It's like the fantasy of flying, of being invincible." He brings the thickshake over to where I'm standing at the sink and sits on the kitchen bench next to me. He says, "When I'm alone and thinking about the way your Mum has taken the place of my Mum, then sometimes I get angry with you, Jenny. I know it's got nothing to do with you. But just *knowing* something like that doesn't always help. Then I write in my *CASEBOOK*: cold stuff about you and your Mum."

Tristan is silent for a while, staring into his thickshake as if all the answers to all the questions in the universe are to be found in a glass of chocolate milk. Then he says, "When I'm with you, Jenny—like now—I don't feel that way at all. I feel ashamed of what I've written. You're, you know, warm and human."

"Thanks," I say, feeling uncomfortable but pleased.

"But you get these fantasies too, Jenny."

"Well, not quite like yours," I say sharply.

"That story you were telling me—the one about the guy calling you from another time. That's the same sort of thing. It's a fantasy about having secret friends, about power, about controlling the present and the past."

"Crap," I say. A bit of potato flies across the room.

"It *is*, Jenny. I've read lots of books about this sort of thing. I discussed it endlessly with Dr. Grogan—you know, my analyst, my *shrink* as you'd call her. There's nothing wrong with having fantasies—but you've got to learn from them. You've got to face the real-life problems that the fantasies are compensating for—"

"That's a load of crap, Tristan. I'm sorry to tell you this, but you're raving."

"Jenny," he says patiently, "believe me, there's this phenomenon called *resistance*."

"I know all about resistance, thank you very much, you measure it in Ohms."

"Not electrical resistance. Psychological resistance. It is a bit similar, I suppose. You are refusing to see that all this telephone stuff is really about...."

"Look, smartarse, I get all this crap from my science teacher, Mrs. Levine. She thinks my telephone story is really about me wanting to change history so that my Mum doesn't go off and marry your Dad. You think my telephone story is about me wanting to be all-powerful and have secret friends who can control the universe. Well, you're both wrong. The point about my telephone story is that it isn't a story. It's true."

"I see. It's true."

"Very, very true. I've got this mate called Rod Gianforte and he calls me up from 1960. Regularly. So there."

There's silence in the kitchen for a while. I realize I've been almost shouting at Tristan. But it is a real relief to have told somebody openly about Rod. It was all getting bottled up inside. I look at Tristan to see if he believes me. He doesn't. He thinks I'm a fruitcake.

"Jenny," he says very quietly, pronouncing every word very clearly, "I know about this trip. I've been there. When I first cracked up I really believed my own fantasies. Just like you now believe...."

"Don't talk to me like that!" I yell at him. "You're talking like I was an imbecile or someone who can't speak English very well. Talk normally."

"Sorry," he says, and returns to his usual rate. "But what I'm saying is true. It is impossible to call the past."

"It's not the past, it's the future."

"I thought you said this guy Rod was in 1960."

"He is. So when he rings me up, he's ringing up the *future*—see?"

"And he's a real person? Not just someone you've made up?"

"Absolutely. It might sound weird. It is weird. But it's true."

"So let's ring him up. Now. I'd love to talk to this guy myself; ask him a few questions."

"We can't. He has to ring me."

"Ah, I *see*," says Tristan, like he's humoring a particularly difficult child. "You haven't got quite enough control over this all-powerful device to be able to demonstrate it to a third party?"

"It needs a bloody great machine," I shout. "A resonance generator. Rod's invented it. Not me. He's got the machine at *his* end, in his time. And it won't be in resonance again until tomorrow afternoon."

"Ah, yes. It figures. Tell me, Jenny, how do you *know* that this isn't all a delusion on your part? How do you know it's true?"

"Because it bloody well is!"

"But you've got no proof?"

"Rod tells me stuff he only knows because I tell it to him after he's told it to me. Davy was there too. See?" It doesn't sound very sensible as it comes out of my mouth, but that's the trouble with time loops.

"No, I really don't see," Tris says sadly. "This doesn't sound very convincing, Jenny. If you think about it, it sounds a bit mad. How do you know you're not imagining all this?"

I don't say anything. There is nothing I can say. If I try to tell him anything, he'll just say that there is no way of knowing that I'm not stark raving bonkers. I just go on peeling potatoes. I discover that I've peeled enough potatoes to feed ten people. I feel a bit of a fool.

"You haven't drunk your thickshake," Tristan says.

It's true. I've peeled a thousand potatoes without drinking a drop. I down the thickshake in three big gulps. I'm beginning to feel a bit vulnerable. After all, how do I actually know that Rod is real? How do I know that the whole thing *isn't* just a figment of my imagination?

Then an idea occurs to me. It's so obvious I wonder why I haven't done it already. "Look," I say, "I'll tell you what I'll do. I'll record the next conversation I have with Rod. Okay?"

"That would be very interesting, Jenny. I'd love to hear a tape of someone talking in 1960—a tape that was made in 1995. Although it'd be more impressive the other way around."

Tristan is still talking to me as if I'm mad. I know what he's thinking: he's thinking that the tape will confirm his loony theories about me being in the grip of a fantasy that I can't distinguish from reality. I suppose he thinks I'm going to concoct the tape myself: put on a gruff voice and pretend to be a man when I'm acting out Rod's part of the conversation. Well, Tristan's got another think coming. Rod sounds like *Rod*. He certainly doesn't sound like a fourteen year old girl pretending to be a man.

Suddenly I want to be alone for a bit. I start to regret asking Tristan to stay for tea. He and Poppa will have to meet one day—but I'm feeling a bit worn out. Just at the moment, I could do without the emotional strain of playing hostess at a step-brother-meets-step-sister's-father tea-party.

Maybe Tristan feels the same thing. He actually is quite a sensitive boy. "Look, I think I'd actually better go, Jenny. I've got stacks of homework—mathematics, English, Society and the Environment, you name it."

"Yeah, all right," I say. "I'll see you to the door."

As he disappears into the early evening, Tristan says, "Don't forget to make that tape."

"I won't, buster," I yell at his retreating back.

I shut the door. Actually, I think to myself, it would be great to have a recording of Rod—something real and tangible that I could play over and over—not just a voice that comes out of nowhere on the phone. It'd be great to have a recording for all sorts of reasons, not just because Tristan needs convincing. I go into Poppa's study and get his Dictaphone. When Poppa arrives home a few minutes later I'm in the hall doing a practice recording: holding the Dictaphone up to a 005 number I've rung.

"Jenny dear, what are you doing?"

"Recording Dial-a-Prayer," I explain.

"Sweetie, what on earth for?"

"Homework. Society and Environment. Other people's beliefs."

"It wouldn't have happened in my day." Poppa goes through into the kitchen, shaking his head. Half a minute later he yells,

"What in tarnation are all these potatoes doing?"

"We're having potato soup," I call back as I'm putting down the phone.

"There's enough to feed an army."

"That's why we've got a deep-freeze. We can have potato soup once a week for months."

In my hand the tape starts to issue its orders to God: "Dear Lord, help us to grow in spirit and in wisdom. Give us the courage to overcome adversity. Make us...."

SUNDAY, 7 MAY, AFTERNOON

Really, there's only one way I'm going to convince Tristan that I'm not hallucinating, or inventing some wild story to make myself sound interesting. I do need to tape-record my next conversation with Rod. Poppa doesn't want me to use his Dictaphone because he depends on it for work, not as if I'd be likely to break it or anything, but that's the way he thinks. So I search through an old Tandy catalogue to see if they sell those magnetic resonance things you see undercover detectives using on cop shows to bug calls. You clip it on the phone line near the handset, then run a wire back to your tape recorder. It's probably illegal. I can't find any ads for it, anyway, and in any case I wouldn't be able to get one until the shops open on Monday but Rod's due to call me back this afternoon. Any minute, in fact. I try propping the tape deck next to the ear-piece, because it's got its own miniature built-in mike, but the rotten thing keeps tipping over or I slip and drop the phone. What I need is a separate microphone with a cord and a jack on the end. I ring Davy.

"Hi, Jen. Watcha doing?"

"Hi, David. Your Dad's got a classy reel-to-reel tape machine, doesn't he?"

"Huh?"

"You know, the one he uses to record his old cronies when they get together to play jazz." Oomp-pa, oomp-pa. I hate trad jazz, and so does Davy, which is one reason we mostly see each other around here instead of at his folks' place.

"Yeah. Oh, yeah, the stereo mike. Do you want to borrow it? He'll go off his face."

"Can you sneak it out and bring it over?"

"I never knew you were musical, Jen."

"This is to record off the phone."

Davy draws in his breath suspiciously. "Is that creep still ringing you? I thought it must have been Tristan, mucking around. It's not, is it?"

"What? Of course not. Don't be ridiculous. Can you get it or not?"

"Okay. I thought you were pissed off at me."

"That's silly. Look, hurry, can you?" Rod could call any time.

"Five minutes."

Luckily Poppa is off at one of his dreary weekend conferences (unless he's got a new girlfriend, ha ha) so Davy gets in the front door without a lengthy and painful attempt at conversation. He's got this big fat mike in a plastic bag. I prop it on the table where we keep the phone and the message pad and plug it into my Sanyo.

"Testing, testing."

Amazingly, it works when we talk into it, but that doesn't mean it will be able to pick up Rod's voice from the phone. I tie it on to the handset with a length of string and punch Maddy's number. Her mother answers, sighs at my name, calls down the hallway for her daughter. "She's doing her geography assignment, Genevieve, so please don't distract the girl. It's hard enough to get her to do any work at home. I don't know how you kids ever get any homework done, you're always on the phone or out mucking around." But she says it with a smile in her voice. I like Mrs. Smith a lot.

"You forgot to turn it on," Davy hisses. He's right, damn it. I push the REC button and the PLAY button together, and the cassette starts to turn. The microphone is heavy, industrial strength, and keeps sliding down the handset away from the ear-piece.

"—your bike ride with Tristan yesterday?" Maddy is babbling

when I get it back to my ear.

"What?"

"I thought you were going to invite me as well." She really sounds disappointed.

"Are you soft on Tris?" I ask teasingly. "Are you going to go all mooshy and clucky when you see him? Are you always going to let him win when you play on the machines at the Arcade?"

"I did not!" Maddy cries indignantly, but I don't believe her. I'm trying to keep one eye on the recording indicator, which is flickering in a suspicious fashion.

"Look, I'm recording this, just hang on for a mo while I check it out." I put down the handset and stop the tape and run it back and then hit PLAY. My own voice comes booming out, but Madeleine's is scratchy and distant and missing bits. This isn't going to work.

"It's not working," I say to Maddy when I pick up again. We have the usual confused exchange and finally I get through to her what I'm trying to do. That girl can be quite thick some-times.

"Oh, is that all you're doing," she says. "What's wrong with the answering machine?"

Davy is mooching around, bored out of his mind. I stare at him, or through him, astonished at what I've just heard. I stare at the stupid arrangement I've got tied to the handset. Maddy's not the slow one. I am.

"—or does it use some special cheapo cassettes?" Maddy is saying.

"No," I say, flipping up the lid and peering inside the old black answering machine that Poppa is too mean to replace with a call-waiting system. "There's a fifteen-second loop-tape that answers your call, and an ordinary thirty-minute cassette for the messages. I think. Hang on." Amazingly, the tape's the right size for my Sanyo. I pop the lid closed on the answering machine. Unfortunately, I can't get it to go without hanging up and waiting for someone to phone in.

"You're a smart girl, Mads. When I hang up, can you call me

straight back? This is really important."

"I suppose. Mum's staring at me something fierce, but. It'll have to be quick."

"Just to test the system. Half a sec, okay?"

"Listen, when you do, take out the answer loop cassette and swap it with the message tape. Otherwise you'll get the usual stuff about 'This is Dr. Kane's residence.'"

"But how do I get it to record?"

"Aw, Jen, come on. When the phone rings and you pick up, just flip it straight into RECORD MESSAGE mode."

"But it'll turn itself off after fifteen seconds."

"No, it *won't*! That only happens with the loop tape. It should just keep running."

"God." I'm incredibly impressed. "Madeleine Smith, you're a genius."

"Yeah, sure. Look, hurry up, okay? Mum's gunna kill me. I'll call you straight back." The phone clicks.

Davy has gone out to the kitchen by this time, and I can hear him digging around in the cookie jars. The boy has a sweet tooth. I hang up the handset, flip cassettes, switch on the answering machine which lights up its little green light, and untie the stupid string holding Davy's dad's stupid stereo music microphone to the handset. The phone rings. I flip to RECORD and press the start-up button. The red light comes on.

"Maddy?"

"Herodotus. It's an hour later for me. What about you? It should be eleven days."

"Um, the Wednesday before last. That's right, eleven days. This is Sunday the 7th. How can that equal one hour of your time?"

"I'll show you the equations some day when you've got a higher degree. Anyway, let's get back to something simple, like how to change the past. Maybe we can still work out how to use this link without short-circuiting the whole universe."

The red light stays on. As far as I can see, the tape is working fine. Running the call through the answering machine gives

Rod's voice an extra distant and eerie quality, but I can understand him without any trouble.

"Last time you said it was like ripples in time."

"Right. Cause and effect work on one another like interfering waves. Ripples passing through each other. Effects ripple out into infinity, for billions of years, and finally they sort of bounce back off the end of the universe and set up an interference with their causes. Of course they're extremely weakened by then."

"That's the silliest thing I ever heard. The universe hasn't got an end. Unless you mean the Big Bang. Or the Big Crunch, when everything collapses into a huge black hole."

"The Big Bang. My aching head. That's probably exactly what I mean, Jenny. Anyway—"

The man is easily distracted. We'll get nowhere fast if I don't keep him on the straight and narrow. "You're saying your machine sets up these ripples in the phone network."

"Thank you. Precisely."

It's logical and beautiful. I see why Mrs. Levine calls science "elegant." Happily, guessing how it works, I tell Rod smugly, "And they don't leak out. So they don't get weaker and fade out."

He is impressed. "I'll give you a job in my lab. Forget about the higher degree, you're hired without one."

I like anyone who likes a pun, so I snigger. "'Highered,' ha ha. So anyway, these, um, ripples, they go backwards and forwards in time and that's why we can talk to each other?"

"You now know as much about it as I do, kiddo."

"So where's the big problem?"

"The big problem, my bright but not all-knowing pupil, is that we can't afford to mess around with the network. Add or subtract one link in the net and the resonance changes. It's like snapping a string on a violin. Screeches and no music."

"Like, if I help you win Lotto and you build a giant mansion by the sea and get them to put in a new phone so you can talk to all your new friends on it—"

"—the network would be busted, the bubble burst, the

ripples ripped. And we would not now be conversing on such an elevated level of speculative physics."

"Oh." That stumps me. How can you do anything if you're not allowed to do anything? After a while I see a sort of possible answer, and say carefully, "What if you just didn't do anything that affected the phone system?"

"But how could I be sure?"

"You'll have to be very, very sneaky, I guess. Would you like me to look up some racing results from the end of 1960? And a list of all the Melbourne Cup winners. Might take a few days."

"Why not? I'll try a modest wager or two, shouldn't do any harm. In the meantime, I have to find out how one delivers a message to someone who won't be born for another two decades or so. Speak to you soon, kiddo." He hangs up, and I turn off the answering machine.

While we've been talking, Davy has slouched past in a bad mood and gone upstairs to my room. He puts on the Braincase CD I don't like any more, and sings along loudly to it. I decide to just ignore this pitiful bid for attention, and flip the cassette out, switch it to the Sanyo recorder, run it back to the start, and play it back. It's perfect. Well, as perfect as a cheap answering machine can make it, which isn't very, but hearing Rod's voice come out of a tape makes a shiver go down my back. It's hard to explain, but it seems different somehow from just talking to someone who's stuck more than thirty years in the past. Hearing his words locked into magnetic tape is awesome, and scary, and almost impossible to believe.

"Hey, Davy, turn it down a bit," I yell up the stairs. I run the tape back and start listening to it again, all about ripples in time. David comes clumping angrily down stairs and grabs his father's microphone off the table and stuffs it into his plastic K-Mart bag.

"You're no fun sometimes, Jen," he says accusingly. "If it's not nerd-features and his new girlfriend, it's this bloody weirdo on the phone. I don't know why you even bothered to get me to come over."

"I asked you to come over to do me a favor," I say, rather coldly. "Don't you remember? It's not all that long ago. You lent me that microphone you're holding in your hand."

"Yeah, well I didn't know you'd be using it to record Creepy the phone freak." He grabs up the Sanyo with Rod's voice in it, and I go off my face.

"Give that back!" I shriek. "It's important! Sometimes you're so mean, Davy." I wrestle the machine out of his hand and put it behind my back. "Sometimes," I add hurtfully, "you're just so stupid." The moment the words are out of my mouth I wish I'd cut my tongue off, but it's way too late.

Davy just stands there like a sick dog. "Yeah, I know. Not you, though. You're a legend," he says slowly, "you've got a mind like a steel trap. Well, at least I don't spend all day hanging around waiting to talk on the phone to some bent weirdo who pretends he's from another planet or something."

"Another *time*, you idiot," I yell at his retreating back, and when he closes the front door he doesn't even bang it like I would. Before I have a chance to work out if I'm going to have a screaming fit in the privacy of my own hallway, or run upstairs for a good cry, the phone rings.

"Dr. Kane's residence," I say in a very tense voice.

"Well, did you get his voice on tape?" asks Tristan, highly skeptical.

I brighten up instantly. "*Yes!* Listen to this, Tris! I'll just play you the tape, hang on."

Then we both sit there, me in Carlton and him in Kew, and listen to the recorded words of a man speaking to me from another time zone.

TRISTAN'S CASEBOOK:
May 7

The present writer has just heard a most extraordinary recorded phone conversation between the subject and the unknown man she insists upon calling "Rod" or "Herodotus." This was a very unsettling experience, as the nature of the exchange makes it apparent that this "story" is not a complete fabrication after all.

It has been the theory of the present writer that the subject's "story" is no more than a delusionary compensation for certain traumatic incidents in her recent life, especially her mother's impending marriage to the present writer's father. This interpretation follows the accepted doctrine of psychoanalysts of the school of Dr. Sigmund Freud, who believed that most claims of abuse and conspiracy were fantasies "covering up" deep sexual problems and anxieties in his patients. However, it has come to the notice of the present writer that this line of thought is being called into question by many contemporary feminists and experts in "recovered memory." These alternative specialists maintain that many such incidents, most too horrible to record here, are not "fantasies" but actually refer to real events in the past and present lives of patients or "clients."

While the present writer is not yet in a position to evaluate such controversies, it does begin to look at if the subject's intriguing case might be based more extensively in "actual events" than has been supposed. This interpretation would clarify a number of odd remarks made to the present writer during the last several weeks. For example, the subject lapsed into discussing her "story" as if it were actually real during the daring bridge-climbing episode shared with the writer.

In regard to that event: it seems to the present writer that a closer and indeed a warmer bond was established with the subject on that occasion. Even though my analyst was furious when I told her that I had, as she put it, "risked my neck in a suicidal gesture," I do not believe that I was trying to kill myself. On the contrary, as I explained to Dr. Grogan, I was merely "showing off" in a typical macho fashion, as my brother Alain might have done. God, I hate being the youngest one in this family. I know that Mother did not kill herself because she was ashamed of me, but it is so hard to believe it, deep down. No wonder I'm such a nerd. No wonder Davy calls me "Dweeb-head," Oh, yes, I've heard him mumbling to Jenny. But the lovely Maddy doesn't seem to think I'm such a hopeless case. She is beautiful and feisty. I think I must be in love with her. I can't get her out of my mind. I dream about her every night. Maybe Jenny and her telephone accomplice "Rod" are as mad as meat axes, but they have brought me into contact with the delicious Madeleine Smith, and for that I shall be eternally grateful.

The present writer notes that he has been "babbling on the screen" for the last five minutes, and will decide later whether or not to delete this file.

MONDAY, 8 MAY, EVENING-A

The TV news is telling us all about the New Europe, and then about the plans the Russian and American Presidents are setting up to deal with joint defense arrangements. "A further round of massive strategic arms reductions appears imminent," says Mary Kostakidis, who's done something weird to her hair. Poppa comes clunking down the hall and drops a mess of files on the kitchen table where I'm finishing off my algebra homework. He gives me a kiss on the back of the head.

"Evening, honey. How'd you like to go out for dinner?"

"I already made a curry, Poppa, it'll be ready in half an hour. Wanna help me slice up some side dishes? You can make the pappadums, too." I close my own folder. My father pours himself a glass of Morris Blanc Superior from the cask in the fridge and throws in some ice.

"You're a good girl, Genevieve. I wish to God your parents had been as thoughtful."

"Um, Poppa, has Mum said anything to you?"

"About what, princess?" He's got his nose in the curry pot. "Hmm, smells wonderful. Have you got a cucumber?"

"Bottom tray of the fridge. I got some of that creamy yoghurt. Um, after the wedding, about her and—" Just keep pushing. What else can I do?

"Jenny, I spent half the morning on the phone to her lawyer. I'm afraid she's decided that she wants to change the custody arrangements."

All over my chest the skin feels cold and horrible. "She wants me to live there with that *creep*?"

"It seems so. Only part of the time, mind you. It seems a quite equitable arrangement, in all truth. Ouch! Damn it, now I've cut my— Jenny, speaking of talking all day on the phone, I tried to ring you for nearly an hour this afternoon. No, no, don't fuss, it's just a small cut." It seems to be bleeding all over the cucumber, but he puts his hand under the cold tap while I get out a Band-Aid, tear off the cover, start its ends, and pass it to him. He hates anyone fussing about pain. "You really have to stop using the phone as your private line to your friend David."

"It wasn't David. We've had an argument."

"Well, whomever. I needed to speak to you."

"Here I am," I say grumpily.

"Hmm. So you are. Genevieve, I received a most extraordinary document in the mail today."

Instantly, in a flash of delight that burns through my whole body and pushes out all the sick feelings about Mum's impending marriage, I realize what it means. I can't believe it, but I know it's got to be true. "Oh shit," I blurt. "It really worked."

Poppa doesn't notice. "I've got it here in my coat. I must say I've never heard of these people. A firm of solicitors in New York, evidently, representing something called the Ripple Corporation."

"A million dollars," I breath. Ripple. Oh my God.

"Eh?" He looks up sharply. "Don't be absurd, child. Still, it's nearly as impressive. I really don't understand it. I've spoken to your Principal and she doesn't understand it either."

The real world intrudes with a jolt. "Huh? What's old Blakers got to do with it?"

"Genevieve, show some respect. In fact, Mrs. Blakeley knows nothing about it."

"About *what*? Tell me, Poppady, or I'll give your curry to the cat."

"We don't have a cat. It's a scholarship, evidently. Your excellent marks have attracted the attention of an educational founda-

ZONES | 145

tion in the United States. A bursarship has been granted which will see you through any university in the world, assuming your final marks are up to scratch. There's a most generous living allowance. In the meantime, you are allotted two thousand dollars a year toward science research materials. Jenny, have you decided to go into science?"

"Poppa, I've been in the advanced phys/maths stream for two years." I can hardly get any air into my lungs. "Oh boy. Oh wow. New York, here I come!"

"Slow down, princess." But he's smiling too, grinning with shared delight. "Not for a few years yet."

"What's a few years?" I grab up the letter and dance around the kitchen, school heels clattering on the tiles. "What's time? It's just...just *ripples*, Poppa!"

§

The phone rings once, and I've got it.

"Dr. Kane's residence."

"If all my planning worked out," Rod says in a tautly controlled voice, "you should now be a few pounds better off— dollars, I mean."

"Rod, thank you. You're wonderful! I believe every word!"

"I don't see why you should. I could still be a wealthy name-less telephone mugger with a confederate in Sydney."

"Why Sydney? The Ripple Corporation is in New York."

"Oh? Things must be going to work out really well. I set it up with a lawyer who was at Sydney University with me back in the Dark Ages. That's just a start, Jenny. We'll be placing your half of the earnings in an investment portfolio to be delivered into your hands when you turn twenty-one. I think you should be mature enough by then to know how to handle, uh, how should I put it, he-he, *incredible wealth*."

But I don't giggle along. I can feel my mood shifting as his becomes more manic. "Rod," I say, and stop, sucking at my lower lip.

After a moment he says back, "Jenny."

"Rod, I've been wondering about this. We shouldn't use it just for ourselves. This is too important."

"Well, think of it as an experimental test. Normally you'd use strings of random numbers. So why not use horse races and make some money on the side?"

"I think we should save those poor people in the Shuttle."

"The what?"

"There was a mini-series on TV. Seven astronauts got killed when the space shuttle blew up in 1986. It was a fault in the O-rings. I mean, the technicians *knew* there was a problem, but no one listened to them. But if you sent them a letter in, say, 1984 or 1985, they'd have to investigate it, wouldn't they? You could stop the *Challenger* taking off."

"The O-...? Jenny, hang on. I don't even know what this shuttle thing is—"

"It's a space ship! There were two women on board! I mean, one of them was just a school teacher, and they—"

Rod cuts over me. "I'm sorry to hear that, kiddo. Tragic. But Jenny, why stop there? There must have been worse disasters in the last thirty-five years."

He's right. I keep forgetting how *far back* he's talking from. They didn't even *have* shuttles. My God, they hadn't even landed on the Moon. No wonder he got weird when I mentioned the Apollo program. And there were those nutty questions about Kennedy and Nixon— "Oh golly. When did you say you were ringing from?"

"It's October 12, 1960."

"In about three years, President Kennedy is going to be shot."

"Jesus! Assassinated?" He's shocked into silence. "Is that how Nixon—?"

"No, that was later. You've got to stop it happening, Rod. Maybe we could stop the Vietnam War before it starts."

"Jenny, Jenny, that's the whole problem!" I hear anguish in his voice, real adult horror and suddenly I feel like a silly kid, and I hate it. "How could I? How long do you think I'd stay out of jail if I phoned the American Embassy and said, "Hey, chaps, President Kennedy's going to be killed in 1963'? He's not even *president* yet!"

In a sulky tone I say, "So what? You haven't even put any money on those horses yet, but my father's already got the scholarship from your lawyers. I haven't even looked up the winners, for heaven's sake!"

"Hmm. But don't you see, that *won't happen* if I stop Kennedy's murder. In your world, Kennedy's dead. I have to leave it that way, or the resonance is destroyed. The link is broken. None of this will have ever happened. Not even our first phone conversation."

"I don't care. Poppa has enough money, I don't need your scholarship. I think we should—"

"Jenny, calm down." He doesn't sound very calm himself. "I don't say I disagree with you. But why stop with one man's death? Haven't there been other disasters?"

My mind goes blank. All I can think about is TV news broadcasts. "Uh, there was that earthquake in Afghanistan, and, um, the famine in Rwanda because of the war—"

"We can't stop an earthquake or a war, kiddo. I don't think anyone would believe us anyway, so we couldn't even get the place evacuated."

"Three Mile Island! It was a nuclear accident in the States."

"An atomic accident! My God! How many killed? Hundreds of thousands, I suppose."

"I don't think anyone was *killed*, exactly. But it nearly melted-down, like Chernobyl."

"Where's that?"

"Some part of what used to be the Soviet Union."

"*Used* to be?" Rod is utterly incredulous. "Are you saying that communism isn't— God, the far right are going to love that. No one, I mean *no one*, will believe any of this! I mean it. Who would believe us, Jenny?"

"Bhopal! That was really awful! We could stop that."

"Somewhere in India?"

"Just a tick, I've got the Yearbooks here. Capital of Madhya Pradesh, however you pronounce it. December the third—"

"1994?"

"No, way back, 1985, I must have still been in kindergarten but Mrs. Levine goes on and on about it, it's stuck in my memory. Methyl iso-kyan-ate...."

"Iso-*sigh*-an-ate."

"...a deadly gas used for making pesticides, leaked out of a... Union Carbide.... Many residents died in their sleep, 2,500 dead, many thousands more blinded. Rod, it was really *horrible*! We could stop that, couldn't we? All we have to do is tell them to check their storage tanks. Rod, there were *babies*!"

His voice is absolutely flat. "We can't."

"Why not?" I'm literally hopping up and down, and the phone cord is banging on the wall. "It's our duty!"

He sighs bleakly. "Look, think this through, kiddo. Sure we can change your past, my future, whatever you want to call it— *but we can only do it once*! One shot. Then the resonance is disrupted, and our time zones drift off in different directions."

For some reason I think of my mother, sitting there in the leafy garden of Edward's house in Kew with only Tristan the dweeb and Lamb Chop the killer dog for company, instead of her own daughter. "We'll never talk to other again?"

"Worse. None of this will have ever happened. We never *did* speak to each other."

It makes me feel sick as well as disoriented. Flippantly, to hide it from him and me, I say, "There goes your Nobel Prize. Not to mention all the millions."

"We've already established that I'm not going to get a Nobel Prize. Not in the next thirty-five years, anyway."

"Well, you've certainly become *some* kind of big shot." I'm starting to feel desperate and sad. I pick up the brochure from the table, I haven't even read it properly yet. "Listen, here's this thing they sent along with my scholarship letter, it probably lists you as chairman of the board."

"I don't think so. I'm planning to be very discreet." After I've been silent for a time, he says, "Well?"

I'm such a baby. I feel as if I'm going to burst into tears again. And I've never even *met* this guy, and by now he'd probably be old enough to be my grandfather. "Oh gee. Oh Rod, I'm so sorry.... I didn't have time to read it before—"

"What's wrong?"

"Oh, it's nothing. I was looking at the wrong bit. Hey, this is interesting, there are no phone numbers listed for the Corporation, just an address and a box number in New York—"

I don't fool him. Forcefully he says, "Tell me, Jenny. It's something about me, isn't it?"

"You don't want to know." I don't want to know. "You've just said you can't change time."

"Of course we can change time. You would never have got that bloody letter if we couldn't change time. Read it to me. You owe me that much."

"Oh, Rod!" The tears are leaking down my chin. "It says, 'The Ripple Corporation is a non-profit organization established under the laws of New Jersey as an educational and research fund.'"

I'm reading very clumsily, getting everything tangled with my thick tongue. I stop, swallow, try again. "'It rewards accomplishment in many fields of science and the arts. What is more, in keeping with the founder's far-sighted belief in the future, the Ripple Corporation seeks out bright young talent and encourages—' Rod, I can't read this to you."

"The *founder*? That's me? God, they make me sound like I'm a thousand years old. Or as if I'm—" He stops dead.

"That's what it says here, Rod. 'His own painful search for truth, which cost his life.' There's something about synchrotron radiation. Do you know what that is?"

"Oh Jenny." His voice is a thousand kays away, and right in my ear. His voice sounds *gray*. "I feel sick. I think I'm going to *be* sick. Just a moment.... My own obituary. God, I feel as if I'd been smashed in the guts." I hear him take a deep breath. "When do I die?"

"They don't say. No, here it is. 1935-1963. Oh Rod, you're going to die the same year as President Kennedy."

"A macabre note of distinction, Jenny. My God, three years. No, it's not true. I can't believe it." It's as if I can hear his brain roaring, a motor for thinking impossible ideas. Then he says, "It's the resonance. It must be. But I don't feel sick. 1963. McReady and I have only been using the machine for a few weeks. If I shut it down right now...."

"You have to, Rod! It's killing you! Do it, turn it off."

"You haven't researched the race winners yet, Jenny. If I shut the machine down I'll never win that money and never start the Ripple Corporation and you'll never have got that brochure.... This is crazy. We really are talking about altering the future. The past."

Hotly, I say, "Well, if you think I'm gonna go ahead and tell you those race results, now I know it'll kill you—then *you're* the one that's crazy!"

"Jenny, you're right. Unless I can find some way to shield the machine."

Neither of us says anything for a while. I realize suddenly how dark it is in the hallway, and reach over to switch on the light.

"If you do," I say at last, "you know how to reach me."

"If you're still in the same future, Miss Steel Trap." Another pause which neither of us can fill. "You know, I've really got quite fond of you. I wish I had a sister like you. A daughter."

"Are you married?"

"Not yet."

"I'm going to hang up now, Rod," I say very definitely. "I hope you don't die."

"Thank you, kiddo." His voice is faint, and choked. "This is like two ghosts saying goodbye to each other. Look after yourself."

"Bye, Rod."

I cradle the phone before he does. Then I just sit there for a long time, hunched over the useless thing, sobbing like a baby.

MONDAY, 8 MAY, EVENING-B (REVISED WORLD)

The TV news is telling us all about the New Europe, and then about the plans the Russian and American Presidents are setting up to deal with nuclear defense arrangements. "A further round of massive strategic arms reductions appears imminent," says Mary Kostakidis, who's done something weird to her hair.

"I want all this junk off the table pronto, young lady."

"It's not junk, Mum, it's my science project."

"I know, sweetie, but we have to get the table set. What's wrong with your own desk?"

"It's covered in junk. Gosh, a *lace table-cloth*? We are getting fancy."

"Oh, your father wants to make a big impression," my mother says, shooing me away. "Now go and get ready, I want you on your best behavior tonight."

"Aw, yack yack yack about economics and balance of payments all night."

"Actually, you might even learn something. Our guest is a physicist from the States. Your father was on the debating team with him at Sydney University."

"I thought physicists were the Enemy of the Department?"

"This one is the biggest Enemy of them all, which I think is why your father is hoping to butter him up, aulde acquaintance and so on."

"Oh. Is he the one all the fuss was—"

"Little pitchers have big ears. Not a word about that. The University was very lucky to get Professor Kanthamani. Berkeley was quite eager to keep him, apparently, but he wanted to come back to Australia. God knows why he chose Melbourne."

I pick at the shiny black olives piled in a bowl. "Poppa won't be in a very good mood, then. I can remember him ranting on about—"

"Genevieve! Your father never rants. He might *sulk* a little...."

She's *always* criticizing. I butt in, "So what happened to what's-his-name, the last guy we had to dinner?"

Mum is snide, and I don't know why. "I greatly admire the precision which a mathematical education brings to the mind of the young."

"Oh, that distinguished-looking man, you know, from Deakin's Business Administration. You and him were laughing all night."

My mother's eyes narrow. There is a clatter of silverware. "Money's tight, sweetie, especially in universities. It's some-thing you won't understand until you're a few years older. If one wishes to acquire a certain tasty plum, according to the Vice Chancellor, one has to forego another. It's a matter of balance, Jenny, a matter of juggling and compromise."

She's getting very snaky these days. In a sudden bad mood, I tell her, "I don't care if he *is* a physicist, I'd rather go over to Maddy's for tea. We can finish our homework together."

Mum seems more pleased with this idea than I'd wish, somehow. I think she enjoys getting a bit soused at dinner parties and flirting with the guests, but feels it's a bad influ-ence on her suggestible teenage daughter. "Oh, I suppose we can spare you," she says carelessly. "Just this once. But you'd better call her mother first and check."

I grab up my text books, drop the pile on the hall table, punch the number. A lot of noisy headbanger stuff comes through the line when it's finally answered.

"Hi, Maddy. Listen, can you ask your Mum—" Behind me,

competing with the heavy metal in my ear, Mum is calling firmly, "Just don't hang on the phone for hours, Jenny. You spend far too much time hogging that instrument." I just grin, and get down to the serious business of quizzing Madeleine about her hunky boyfriend David. Then it turns out they're already booked for the night, so I'm stuck at home.

§

Dinner starts off as a nightmare, a real pain. This Professor Kanthamani is about Poppa's age, but he looks younger. He's chubby and dark, with thick waving hair that looks as if he's poured oil all over it, and he is rather lofty and dignified. Mum is put out because he's brought a bottle of some awful red wine and insists that she open it, even though she's serving chilled Chablis with the chicken. He and Poppa stumble through dry conversations about economic rationalism and the terrible things the Vice Chancellors are doing to academic freedom, but I can tell neither of them has his heart in it. Mum just seethes.

And then something wonderful happens. Prof Kanthamani starts telling us about an amazing quantum theory experiment that's just been done at the University of California at Berkeley, in the USA. It's all about time. Somehow, it seems that what we do *now*, at this very moment, can change things in the *past*. I listen to this with my eyes bulging and my mouth open.

"Genevieve, close your mouth," Mum says, "a fly will get in."

"There are no flies on Jenny," Poppa says. "She's just dazzled by science."

I gulp, and a bit of chicken goes down the wrong way, and then I'm coughing and spluttering. The scientist leaps up and pours me a glass of water and everyone looks very concerned, and I say, "Do you really mean that we can change the past, Dr. Kanthamani?"

Maybe my interest in science cheers him up, because he smiles warmly at me for the first time all night.

"Call me Ram, Jenny, everyone does eventually. Short for Rambo, because I'm named after a famous movie star, which is why I went into physics. Just joking." Strange sense of humor if you ask me, but I give him a careful grin. He takes back the glass and asks, "Feeling better?"

I cough one last time, and find that I can breathe again.

"Yeah, thanks. Is that right, though, about time?"

"Not exactly," Ram says. He glances at my parents. Mum shrugs, Poppa nods interestedly. "What Raymond Chiao's experiments have shown is that bits of the past aren't totally completed until the present moment occurs—or even until the future happens. Oh dear, I've made it worse. It's hard to talk about this kind of thing in ordinary English, our language isn't built for temporal paradoxes."

Poppa pours another glass of Ram's cheap claret and sips it without wrinkling his nose at the taste. "But Ram, how can this quantum experiment be a paradox if you can test it in the laboratory? A paradox is an error of language, like asking who shaves the barber if the barber only shaves those who can't shave themselves."

Barber who *what*? I think.

"*Ms.* Barber," Mum says snidely, "she does it." Both the men laugh.

"That's cheating," Ram tells her. "The logical trick—it's called Russell's Paradox, as I recall—depends on the barber being a man with his own shaving problems. So who shaves him, if he can only shave those who can't shave themselves? And no, Jenny, he doesn't nip out of town to get it done somewhere else, and he isn't allowed to grow a beard."

My head spins a bit as I try to think it through. "I dunno, Ram. Sounds impossible."

"It's a trick of words," Poppa declares. "Don't the philosophers call that 'self-reference'? One part of the puzzle looping back to undermine an earlier part? Really, valid logic doesn't allow you to do that. It's like lifting yourself into the air by tugging at the soles of your shoes." I *almost* see what he means, but Mum is just shrugging her shoulders at the stupid games men play. She heads out into the kitchen to prepare dessert. I get up to collect the plates.

"The quantum eraser experiments aren't like that, though," Ram says. Now that he's on his own topic he's happy as a lark, relaxed and ready to talk all night. I grab his empty plate and put it on top of Poppa's, and then loiter in the doorway to the kitchen because I don't want to miss any of this. "Actually, if you want the full low-down on this kind of caper, you should chase up my old mate Rod Gianforte—if you can find him. He was heavily into quantum weirdness twenty or thirty years before it became fashionable."

"Rod Gianforte?" Poppa says, scratching his head. "Wasn't he at Sydney university in the early sixties? Some terrible scandal about a ruined computer?"

"Yeah. Went out with a bang—I don't think they've ever forgiven him. Lucky to get a job in some small sheep college in New Zealand. Actually I gather he's back in Australia these days—lurking somewhere in Newtown, I imagine."

There's the weirdest buzzing in the top of my head, as if I'm going to faint, or lift off my feet into the air even without tugging at the soles of my shoes, or something else totally impossible, I don't know. Suddenly I get the most awesome feeling that I *already know* this guy Prof Ram. Or maybe the one he just mentioned, Rod something-or-other. I'm absolutely convinced that we've talked about all this before, and that—

What? I just don't know. It's called *déjà-vu*, I think—the sensation that something has happened before, exactly like this moment now. You walk into a room where you've never been before and instantly recognize all the furniture, and the paintings on the walls, and you know in your bones that outside in the yard there's a huge oak tree with a rubber tire for kids to swing on hanging from a chain, and a brown bantam hen scratching and...

Only that's not it, not precisely. I don't think this *exact same dinner* has happened before, or that it's actually Ram Kanthamani

I'm remembering. Mum calls crabbily to me to bring the plates and cutlery in to the dishwasher, and I'm standing here in the doorway numb from the neck down, wondering if I'm going to barf. This *has* happened before! No! No, something else—

"In Ray Chiao's experiment," Prof Ram is saying, "single photons are sent through a beam-splitter—"

"Photons?" asks Poppa. He knows all about running the economy, but physics is just a black hole for him and Mum.

"Particles of light," says Ram. I put the plates into the open dishwasher without bothering to rinse them, and shoot back into the room. I don't want to miss any of this.

"Particles? I thought light was made of waves," Poppa says, even more confused. "Light-waves."

Ram looks very pleased with himself. He pounces.

"Exactly! Sometimes it's a wave, but at other times it looks like a stream of little hard pellets."

"Don't be ridiculous, Ram," Poppa says crossly. "That really *is* a paradox." He takes a piece of fruit out of the bowl in the middle of the table and brandishes it in the air. "It's like saying this apple is red and green at the same time."

"Dear, it is," Mum tells him, coming back into the room with several plates of apple cream flan balanced along her arm like a waiter. "Look more closely. It's red on the top where it's ripest, and green underneath."

"No, no," cries Prof Ram excitedly. "Dr. Kane is right, quantum effects *are* paradoxical, by ordinary standards—as if that apple were both *all* green and *all* red at one and the same time." Poppa opens his mouth to interrupt, but Ram wags a finger under his nose. "Let me tell you about Chiao's experiment. You see, they send a single photon through a— No, wait on, let me try my little 'quantum eraser' story on you. That's where you rub out the past and then get it back again by changing your mind later."

Now we're all staring at him with our mouths open. "Colored lines will make it easier," he adds. "This is a parable I dreamed up for my students." He grabs a piece of paper from the sideboard, digs out one of the five or six felt-tipped pens jutting from his inside suit pocket, and starts drawing diverging lines in different colors.

"I told you science had become the new religion," Mum says snidely. "'Parables,' indeed."

Ram isn't put off. "Imagine there's a huge bunch of football players, and just before they run on to the field they're randomly divided into two teams with distinctive colors."

"Ah," says Mum, "a male chauvinist parable!"

"Not at all!" He laughs in a lilting, Indian way. "The womenfolk are welcome, for these are non-sexist teams! Men and women in equal numbers."

I can see Mum about to go ballistic when she hears such a vile term as "womenfolk" but she catches herself in time, realizing that Ram is pulling her leg.

"Could we just have colors by themselves, without the allegorical football players?"

Ram shrugs. "Very well. I do not know any women footballers anyway." He loses his pens and grab frantically for them as they roll off the table. "Let us say that a single photon or light particle is divided into two by a device called, amazingly enough, a 'beam-splitter.' Now you must bear in mind that these colors I am going to draw really aren't colors at all, but just a way of keeping track of what's happening."

He peers at us doubtfully. Poppa nods even more doubtfully. My mother shakes her head in despair, and says, "Clear as mud."

Ram has drawn one line splitting into two thin black lines that spread apart until each of them enters a separate little box, marked TOP and BOTTOM. When they emerge from their boxes, they split once again, but now there are four colors. Coming out of the TOP box is a yellow line heading upwards and an orange line heading downwards, slowly getting further apart from each other. Down below, coming out of the BOTTOM box, there's an upward-heading blue line and a downward purple line. Plus there's a spot where the yellow line at the very top bounces off a mirror and starts heading down again. Is this craziness supposed to make sense?

"What a mess," I say.

"Jenny," Mum says, "that is a rather rude comment. And you haven't touched your pudding."

Ram looks abashed, and takes a quick taste himself. "I'm sorry, Harriet, this sweet is wonderful, the cinnamon is a touch of genius. Am I ruining your excellent meal with my allegory?"

After a long moment's silence, when it becomes obvious that Mum is not going to let him off the hook, Poppa says, "Not at all, Ram, I for one am intrigued. It's not often we have anyone from the sciences here to dinner. Usually the conversation is about funding for the arts—deathly boring." Mum's lips tighten, but Professor Ram has put his spoon aside to go back to his diagram, and starts on again about his quantum splitter or whatever it is.

"Okay, now the Yellow and Blue lines merge." They're the two that were both running toward the top of the page, except the Yellow line bounces off a mirror there and runs down again to cross over the Blue line. "Imagine the Blue and Yellow lines pass under a camera at the intersection."

"A traffic camera," I say, grinning.

"What about the Orange and Purple lines?" Poppa asks.

"Forget them for a moment. They're both running south. Eventually they meet up and merge together, and we never hear from them again. Maybe they run down the page until they fall off the edge of the world." I laugh, because physicists aren't supposed to talk about the world having an edge. But this is just a parable, after all.

"This traffic camera," Mum says. "Presumably it's going to take a picture of the Yellow and Blue lines, which will join together at the intersection, and this will prove that light is either a wave or a particle. Or have I missed something?"

"No, Harriet, you're ahead of me. The camera snaps a single, shot of the two overlapping lines. When it's developed, it shows only a Green blur."

"Because," Poppa says, nodding, "the yellow and blue colors

get mixed together on the exposed film, and that creates this green streak."

"Exactly. Think of that case as light behaving like a wave. Instead of our split photon travelling through the detector in the form of one distinct color or the other, it sort of gets smeared into a blurry wave."

Mum looks up suddenly with her spoon in her mouth. "I remember this now," she says, "atoms and electrons and so forth look like waves or particles depending on how you choose to observe them."

"Correct. So let's change the way we're observing these lines. Suppose we'd blocked one of the two lines running away down the south-bound roads, the Orange and Purple ones. Now we have a way of telling these two lines apart, which we were unable to do before. Say the Purple line is blocked." Ram pauses, and stares at each of us with a strange, mischievous excitement. "This is where it gets bizarre. *Instantly*, way over here on the other side of the page and it might as well be hundreds of kilometers away, the Yellow and Blue lines mysteriously thin out a little. Now the camera can only manage to take a shot of one colored line or the other, not both at once."

Poppa blinks. "As if they stop being spread out like waves and turn into particles?"

Ram scribbles frantically on his diagram, but at this point it looks as if he needs a computer animation to make it clear. "Give the economist a prize. So, let's say, the camera records only the Yellow line."

"You're cheating!" I cry in outrage. "How can blocking one of the *Blue or Purple* lines influence the *Yellow and Orange* ones? Are they all staying in touch somehow?"

"Nope. Absolutely no contact allowed between the Yellow-Orange pair and the Blue-Purple pair after they separate. That's the mystery of it. But wait! There's more!" he cries, like the advertising guy on telly. "If we re-open the road block now so the Blue and Purple lines do mix together after all," scribble, scribble, "the Yellow and Orange lines *instantly* blend back together. Now, as they cross at that intersection, the camera is again recording a green blur."

"This is making my eyeballs dance," Poppa says sadly.

Mum stares hard at the diagram. "Ram, if I follow you, you're saying that the top photons—the yellowish pair, I mean—stay spread out like waves only so long as nobody can tell one of the bottom photons—the bluish pair—from the other?"

"Precisely. What happens to the *yellowish lines* all depends on whether you make a particular kind of observation about the *bluish lines*, which are completely out of touch with them."

Mum snorts. "Well, that's sounds more like your original football teams. It's always the men who count in the end, and they're always completely out of touch."

Ram shakes his head, and smiles. "This isn't a parable about feminism, Harriet. But look, now it gets *really* weird. Say we re-run the ride once again, but this time we snap the photo of the Yellow and Orange lines crossing *before* anyone has decided whether or not to throw up a roadblock on one of the BOTTOM pair."

I say: "You mean the yellowish lines get photographed while the bluish lines are still running down the page on parallel tracks."

Ram nods. "Right. Then, if you *later* choose to leave the Blue and Purple lines separated, that film you've already taken—without looking at it yet—will show only *one* of the top colors, either Yellow *or* Orange. Remember, my dear, the shot is exposed *before* you decide what to do with the lower colors, but it's developed *after* you carry out that plan. It's as if your decision now in the present has influenced which of the two possibilities the camera recorded in the past."

I stare at him, trembling a little bit. "That's nuts!"

"In the words of my Adelaide colleague Paul Davies," Ram says, not taking offence, "the record of the past remains *undecided*—until we choose later to let the Blue and Purple lines merge, or keep them apart."

The dizziness I felt earlier returns. I'm whirling and buzzing.

What the professor is saying sounds completely insane, but he said it's been done in a laboratory experiment and it works. Changing the past.

Mum has gone quite pale, and I wonder if she's as shocked as I am. "Ram, are you telling me that we can select reality *after* the event? That something I do today can affect what the picture shows even though the camera took it yesterday?"

"Yes, but only if you don't look. Because the past remains undecided until the whole experiment is completed."

I don't know why, but now I really do feel as if I'm going to faint. Or throw up. In a squeaky voice, I ask Ram, "Does that mean we can change the past?"

"Not quite—but the actions we take in the *present moment* help to determine the reality that *was the case* at a past moment. You see, in situations like Ray Chiao's experiment, the present is a kind of double exposure. The past only comes into focus when we—"

But I am losing his voice, which seems to echo and boom at the end of a long corridor. I feel myself slumping back into the chair, sliding gracelessly down on to the floor under the lace table cloth, and the world really has become an overlapping set of different movie frames. Mum is darting around the table to grab my hand, but at the same time she's not even there, not in the room, not even in the house, and Dr. Ram isn't there either, and some nerdish looking boy is holding up something disgusting, I think it's a *human finger*, yuck, cut off at the knuckle, and Maddy's boyfriend Davy is leaning across to kiss me, and Poppa is complaining about me hanging on the phone all the time, and—

TUESDAY, 9 MAY, MORNING (REVISED WORLD)

I'm having this terrible nightmare. My dear old friend has died, and there's nothing I can do about it. Blood everywhere. Ears and fingers cut off, it's horrible. Somehow, in the ridiculous way of dreams, there's a carton of eggs toppling off a bridge and falling down into rocks, and the shells crack open, and I see suddenly that the eggs haven't smashed into runny whites and yellow yolks because they're all hard-boiled, like blind eyes bouncing and jouncing into the water, and there's nothing funny about this, not one little scrap of humor—

I wake up sobbing. My bedroom door opens in the dim light of early morning and Mum bustles in from her upstairs study, where she's been sleeping in the spare bed for the last couple of months. Her warm perfume reaches toward me, and I sit up in bed with tears running down my face and hold out my arms to her like a little scared kid.

"Oh, darling, pet, whatever is the matter?" she murmurs in my ear, hugging me close and stroking my tangled hair. "It's just a bad dream, Jenny, that's all it is."

"I was talking on the telephone," I mumble into her hair, "and then he died."

"It's all right, sweetheart, it's just your imagination playing tricks on you. Nobody's been hurt. There, there."

I realize that I haven't got the faintest idea what I meant. The vague last memories of my dream drain away, and I give myself a shake. Mum sits back and looks at me carefully in the dim light from the shaded window. She pulls out a Kleenex from the pack on the dressing table beside the bed and dabs at my eyes.

"That's better, darling. Now try and go back to sleep, you can still get in another hour's rest before school."

Without quite knowing what I'm about to say, I blurt out: "Mum, are you and Poppa going to get a divorce?"

My mother shoots up off the edge of the bed as if I've jabbed her with a pin, and gazes down at me. "Why, Jenny, whatever gives you such a strange idea? Is that what your dream was about?"

I feel cold all of a sudden, and hunch down under the quilt. "Don't think so. It was about a boy who— I mean a man who—" I stop, my thoughts all tangled. "Well, are you?"

There's a long pause. Then Mum sits down again on the bed and puts her hand on top of the quilt, pressing my shoulder. "It's true that your father and I have been going through a rough patch lately, darling. But—"

I feel a lump in the middle of my chest, and a whiny little snivel comes out my mouth.

"—that doesn't mean we're going to split up," Mum adds firmly. "I know that's happened to a lot of your friends' parents, but it's not going to happen to this marriage. God willing." She leans over, kisses me on the forehead, and stands up again. "Try to get a bit more sleep, darling. You'll see, everything will look a hundred times better when the sun's properly up."

After a while I do drift off to sleep, and when the clock-radio rocks me awake at 7:30 all I recall is waking up from a bad dream, and Mum coming in to comfort me.

§

At lunch, I get a sudden great idea.

"Hey, Mads?"

"You can't have any," she says, greedily holding on to her last slice of pepperoni pizza. "Anyway, I thought you were going on a diet."

"*You're* the anorexic," I say derisively. "No, look, how about you and Davy and me go skating after school? You know, at the ice rink."

Madeleine looks vague for a moment, almost cross-eyed, chewing up her last bit of lunch, and then gives me a big grin. "Absolutely fabulous," she screams like Joanna Lumley on that telly show. "Only one problem—I can't skate."

We fall about laughing. "No troubles, sweetie darling," I shriek back. "There's absolutely nothing to it. Go and tell lover-boy, I'm sure he's got two left feet, he can stop you from falling over and cutting your fingers off." As the words come out of my mouth, a sick jolt of horror goes through the lump of pizza in my guts. Maddy doesn't notice. She just jumps up and zooms across the playground to where the boys are tearing around like great apes.

§

We wobble about on the ice. None of us is particularly good. Maddy has done a bit of roller blading and she reckons ice skating can't be that different, but she still falls over the moment she tries to go fast. Davy wobbles over to help Maddy. She grabs hold of his hand to pull herself up, but only succeeds in pulling Davy down on top of her. They lie on the ice in a giggling heap. I take it easy. I move with little shuffling steps, getting the hang of it, speeding up as I get more confident.

After half an hour all three of us are moving round the ice fairly fast. I dodge between two boys and collide with a third boy who's been catching my eye for some reason. I can't explain it, it's not as if he's especially good looking, or anything. Not like Maddy's boyfriend Davy.

"Sorry," we both say together.

"Snap," says the boy.

I try to think of something witty to say in return. But I can't think of anything. I'm getting these weird feelings again. I feel just like I did when I fainted during Professor Ram's quantum eraser story, or like when I woke up from the nightmare; I feel as if I've been here before, on the ice-rink with this boy. I look at the boy while trying to pretend that I'm not. He's a bit nerdish, wearing a bomber jacket with *Property of the New York Yankees* written on it. I've got this terrible urge to look at his fingers. I'm sure there is something wrong with his fingers, that he's missing one or two. I force myself look at his hands—and there's nothing wrong with them at all.

"Are you okay?" the boy asks. "You look traumatized."

"I'm fine, I'm really fine," I stammer. "Tristan."

His eyes bug and his mouth drops open. "How do you know my name?"

I'm covered in confusion. "I don't know. I just said it. I wasn't meaning to call you anything. Is that really your name? Are you called Tristan?"

"Yeah, that's my name. Have we met before?"

"I don't know," I say. "I suppose we must have. I sort of feel that we've met. But maybe we haven't. Do *you* know *my* name?"

The boy stands there on the ice, thinking. His skates, I notice suddenly, are very expensive, but they look as if he's used them a lot. And his hair's nice. Around us, the other skaters go whirling past. The rock music suddenly stops, and the echoey voice of the disk jockey says, "No throwing snowballs on the ice. Anyone throwing snowballs will be banned from the Ice Arena for the rest of the day." The music starts as suddenly as it stopped. I look around. A couple of kids are discreetly dropping the snowballs they'd made out of the ice-shavings around the edge of the rink. I look back at the boy. He is staring at me hard. I get the impression that he has the same funny feeling that I have. Very seriously he says, "I think you're mad."

I'm grossly insulted. I might be feeling a bit odd, but I'm perfectly sane. I snap back at him, "I'm not remotely mad, thank you very much."

"No, no," the boy says, flustered. "I didn't mean that you are *mad.* I meant that your *name* is Mad. I just had this weird sensation: I've met you before and your name is Mad or Maddy or something."

I gulp. This is truly crazy. "No," I tell the boy, "I'm Jenny. That's Mad over there. The one with the luminous yellow scarf—she's Mad. Madeleine."

The boy looks at Maddy and Davy, who are trying to skate with their arms around each other's waists. Then he looks back at me. "Of course," he says, "you're Jenny. She's Mad. I dunno how I could have mixed you up. But where have we met?"

"Look," I say, "This might sound a crazy question, but have you ever had any trouble with your fingers?"

Tristan stares at me. "No, never. Why?"

"I don't know," I say wretchedly. "I just had this feeling that you'd once lost a finger."

Tristan wriggles his fingers and grins. "All present and correct," he says. I notice that he's tucked his thumb away just to tease me.

"Never had microsurgery?"

"Nope," he says.

And then without thinking, I blurt out. "What about eggs?"

Tristan does a double take. "Eggs?!" he says, "Oh, *eggs.* Well, yeah, I'm not bad with eggs."

He seems to know exactly what I'm talking about, although I don't have a clue what I'm talking about myself. The question just leapt out of my mouth without me knowing what I was asking.

"Look," says Tristan, "Do you want a coffee or something?"

"Yeah, sure," I say.

We both skate over to the rink's exit, stumble in our skates across the rubber matting and through the glass doors into the coffee shop. When we've got our drinks and sit down beside each other at a table, we try to remember where we've met before. We get nowhere. Tristan lives in Kew and goes to some preppy private school. One of his brothers is a famous yachtsman, which just makes me yawn. It doesn't look as if our paths have ever crossed. So I say, "Anyway, about eggs. What are you good at with eggs?"

"You must know," says Tristan. "You asked me about them in the first place."

"Yeah, but I don't know why I asked you. I just did."

"Hang on," says Tristan, "Don't go away."

I watch him disappear in the direction of the lockers. A minute later he comes back with his hands in his pockets. He sits down again at the table, opposite me this time. His right hand goes up to the side of his head as he's reaching for his cooling coffee with his left, and he pulls an egg out of his ear. I smile, but in fact it's pretty easy to see how he does it. He had the egg in his hand all the time, only with the back of his hand turned towards me. It's a pretty amateur performance. He'll have to practice a bit if he wants a job as a magician. But, to be nice, I say, "Great trick. Can you pull one from *my* ear?"

"Anything to please a lady." Tristan turns around quickly in his seat so that I can't see what he is doing, turns back instantly to face me, making a great show of waving his right hand in the air. It's true that nothing appears to be in it. He's genuinely empty-handed. I'm a bit more impressed than I was before. With a flourish he brings his empty hand up to my left ear. But I see what he is up to. I turn my head to get a better look at the egg he is sneaking up to my right ear with his other hand.

Smash. The side of my face goes wet and crunchy. Yuck.

This is really gross. There's raw egg sliding down my face and neck and into the collar of my jumper. My hair is sticking to my ear. A few people at the other tables have witnessed this great feat of the conjurer's art, and there are some cheers and whistles.

Tristan says, "Oops!"

A guy with *Ice Arena—Staff* on his jacket comes over to our table and says to me, "Are you all right?"

"Yeah. Sure. I'm fine. Just fine," I say, seething.

"Well, just watch it, fella," the guy says menacingly to Tristan.

"It was a mistake," Tristan says to the guy. "I thought it was hardboiled. I've got a couple of hardboiled ones in my bag. I must have grabbed the wrong egg."

"Just watch it," the guy says again, but his heart isn't in it, and he wanders back behind the counter.

I go off to the Ladies and clean myself up as best I can. While I'm looking at myself in the mirror, trying to sponge myself down with a wet paper towel, I mutter, "I thought he was better at it than that—a real smooth operator." But why do I think that? I just know I do—I've got this really strong "memory" of Tristan effortlessly producing eggs from people's ears. Hardboiled eggs. Which he then eats. There's a duck floating on a pond. Oh, help! He's balancing on a railing over a massive gorge. Eating an egg. I know where it is: it's Merri Creek. I'm on the pedestrian bridge with him, scared out of my wits. Then I'm back in the Ladies at the Ice Arena. Just standing in front of a mirror with bits of soggy wet paper-towel stuck to my cheek.

When I get back to the Coffee Shop, I'm shaking a bit. Davy and Maddy are just stumbling through the glass doors, wobbly on their hired skates. They see me and I drag them over to meet Tristan. Maddy says something like how Tristan looks familiar, but she doesn't seem to be freaked by the fact: you meet people you vaguely remember all the time, Tristan's no different from the rest. We all drink another round of coffee in styrofoam cups, then go back to the ice.

For the rest of the session the four of us skate around, sometimes as a group, sometimes in pairs, sometimes alone. I decide I want to see more of Tristan, I need to find out what's going on. Before we leave the Ice Arena we exchange addresses and phone numbers.

§

I'd have preferred it if Maddy and David hadn't seen me exchanging addresses with Tristan. They take a keen interest in my love life, Mad and Davy. They are always on about it—or, rather, they are always on about my lack of it. Maddy can get a bit patronizing sometimes. Just because she's got this great hunk David putting his arms round her all the time, she thinks she can lecture me about *lurve* and *passion* and *commitment* and stuff like that. She thinks she's a bit of an expert, truth be told. (To borrow an expression from Poppa.)

David's not much help. He thinks he's god's gift to teenage girls. He thinks he's the reason Maddy thinks she's such an expert. So after we said goodbye to Tristan and got on the train, I know I'm in for a bit of teasing. We are rattling up Swanston Street, past the University, when Maddy says, "Why was your hair all wet in the coffee shop, Jenny? You looked like a drowned rat sitting there without that Tristan guy."

I have half a mind not to tell her. But I want to know if she's been getting these *déjà-vu* feelings as well. So I say, "He bungled the egg trick."

"What egg trick?" David says.

"The one where he pulls a hard-boiled egg from someone's ear and then peels it and eats it."

"Aw yucko," Mandy says. "That's gross."

"Not as gross as when the egg's raw," I say. "And it breaks."

"Is that what he did?"

"The guy's a sicko," David says. "I'd stay clear of him, Jen."

"I rather like him," I say.

"I've heard about getting egg on your face on your first date," Maddy says, "but not before the first date. I reckon if you're still going to go out with a guy after he's carried on in such a *fowl* way—" She winks at me, and I roll my eyes back at her—"well then, it must be true love at first sight. What do you reckon, Davy?"

"Aw, come on Mad. We can find Jen a better specimen than that. There are some cool dudes around. What about—"

"I'm not going *out* with him," I say.

"Yeah, right," Maddy and David say together. Then Maddy says, "No, of course you're not going to go out with him, Jenny Kane. You just gave him your address and telephone number in case he wanted to consult you about his homework, you being such a genius and all that. I mean you wouldn't be interested in going to the movie, or a rage or anything. You just want to talk to him about Fu Manchu and Ming the Merciless."

"What?" Davy says. "What's this Fu Manchu?"

"I don't know," Maddy says. "It's what Jenny talks to boys about."

"She only talks about science, don't you, Jen? Subterranean particles and stuff?"

I'm getting this weird feeling. I say, "Listen, Maddy. Why did you say Fu Manchu and Ming the Merciless? Why did you say I talk about them?"

Maddy looks confused. "It just sort of popped into my head. I reckon that's the sort of thing you and Tristan would talk about. You know, Chinese history. Or maybe it's Japanese."

David says, "Jenny doesn't know anything about Chinese history, do you, Jen?"

"No," I say. "But listen, you two...have we ever met Tristan before?"

"Yeah, right," David says. "Down the loony bin. On the funny farm."

"Come on, be serious," I say. "I've got this sort of memory as being on a bridge with him. I think it's the Merri Creek Bridge. He's fooling around standing on the railing. There's a train rattling past...."

Maddy and David look at each other. David makes a face that says, *Jenny's gone bonkers.* But Maddy looks a bit more worried. I think she knows I'm talking about something serious. She doesn't say anything, just leans across from where she's sitting and puts her hand on my shoulder and squeezes. I know what she means. She means: Let's talk about this when David's not around.

For a moment there's a bit of commotion when a group of Japanese tourists start taking pictures of each other in the aisle of the tram. I start telling Maddy and David about Ray Chiao's experiment. I try to explain it using Dr. Ram's analogy.

I haven't got very far when David says, "Color gangs are all into organized crime in Los Angeles. I saw it on *60 Minutes*. They have shootouts in car parks outside some sleazy bar. Bodies all over the place. And they make half the drugs on the street. Speed and that."

"It's only an analogy about photons, the different colors," I say.

"It's not *analogy*," David says. "It's *analgesic*."

He looks really pleased with his use of a big word, even if he has pronounced it wrong. I tell them that analgesic is another word for aspirin. "But photons," David goes on. "That's a new one. Probably worse than Grievous Bodily Harm. Some of these new drugs—no one knows what's in them. There was this nightclub in Queensland. Everyone was dead by morning."

Maddy just looks out of the window of the tram. I could tell David that photons are actually subatomic particles of light, but somehow, I don't think it's worth the effort. When we get to our stop we all get off the tram and scuttle across to the pavement. I'm meant to go one way and David and Maddy are meant to go the other. But Maddy says, "I'll go home with Jenny."

"Jeez, Mad," David says. "I thought we were both going to your place."

"Yeah, well, I reckon I'd better see Jenny home. She's not feeling well."

"Aren't you, Jen?" David says. He is very concerned. "You should've said. Because I'd of got you an analgesic at the Ice Arena. They're sold in the coffee shop."

"No, it's all right. I haven't got a headache," I say.

"Well, I'll come back to her place, too," David announces. "Then I can walk Maddy back to her place."

"Look, Davy," Maddy says, and puts her arms around him and whispers in his ear. Then she kisses him.

David suddenly seems a bit embarrassed. His face just goes slightly red.

"Oh, um, errr...all right then," he says. "Um, see you later, Jenny."

Maddy kisses him again for about 10 seconds. The pair of them just stand there on the pavement with cars and trucks roaring past and a couple of pedestrians have to walk around them. I exchange a shrug with one of the pedestrians—a woman carrying three plastic bags of shopping and a baby. Then David is disappearing in one direction and Maddy and I are taking the shortcut to my house in the other direction.

"What did you tell him, Mad?"

"What do you reckon?"

"I suppose you told him I had women's troubles."

"Actually, I said *girl troubles.*"

"Same diff," I say.

And then Maddy and I are giggling like kindergarten kids walking along with our arms around each other. Poor David. He's a nice boy and I'm really glad he and Maddy are an item, but the truth is, he's a bit thick. And he'd run a mile from *girl troubles.*

"So what's it all about?" Maddy says as we approach my place. "What's all this about hard-boiled eggs and bridges?"

"Look," I say. "It's just that I've been having these funny flashes."

"Flashes?"

"Here, you know, where one thing remind you of another, and the first thing seems familiar, but it isn't."

"That's just because you forget stuff," Maddy says. "I forget stuff all the time and then maybe I half remember it. School crap especially. Your trouble is that you have a mind like a steel trap. You never forget things. Except now you're starting to. Welcome to the real world."

"No, it's not like that," I say. "I have this feeling I've met Tristan before and he was fooling around on the Merri Creek Bridge. If I'd ever actually had that experience, I couldn't possibly just forget it. Or even half forget it."

"Well, I don't know," Maddy says. "Tristan did sort of seem familiar. And what I said about Fu Manchu—I've got this feeling that Fu Manchu is really the name of Tristan's friend."

"But that's silly," I say. "Nobody is actually called Fu Manchu."

"Must be a nickname."

We've reached our house and we go inside. Nobody is at home. We climb the stairs and sit on my bed.

"Don't worry about it, Jenny," Maddy says. I'm sure there's an explanation. Are you going to go out with the guy?"

"I think I'll go around to his place and see him. Have a talk. See if we can work out what's going on."

"I'd do more than that," Maddy says. "If I were you, Jenny, I'd do a lot more than just *talk* to the boy."

"I know you would."

"It's about time you expanded your horizons."

"*Expanded my horizons*," I say, all innocent. "Why, Madeleine dear, what can you mean?"

"You'll have to find out for yourself."

"No I won't," I say. "You're going to tell me."

And I suddenly turn to where she's sitting beside me on the bed and I grab her under both armpits and tickle her for all I'm worth. Maddy fights back. We roll around giggling for a bit and then she says, "All right, all right, Jenny Kane. I surrender. I'll tell you how to expand your horizons."

And for the next half hour she does just that.

TRISTAN'S CASEBOOK:
May 9

I take up my pen to write in this most sacred of notebooks with less than my usual composure. God, that sounds pretentious. I'm beginning to think that a lot of the crap I write in this notebook *is* pretentious bilge. I'll try to write sensibly.

My brain is out of control. I've met this girl. Jenny. At the Ice Arena. Perhaps Jennifer. But no, I don't think so. I think Genevieve. I'm sure it's Genevieve. I know it's Genevieve. But the question is: why do I know it's Genevieve? She didn't tell me, she just said that her name is Jenny. At first I thought it was Madeleine, but that was her friend. It was weird. And she knew my name straight away. I didn't have to tell her.

I made a fool of myself, though. The egg trick went all wrong. Poor girl. She had yolk and albumen running all down the side of her face and in her hair and everything. I could've crawled under the table I was so embarrassed. She was nice about it, though. And afterwards we were skating together and she was laughing, and, well, when she laughs as she was quite pretty. That's a bit mean, saying she looks "quite pretty." She looked pretty. Full stop. She gave me her phone number and address. Maybe *she'll* ring *me*. But if she doesn't, I'll damn well call her.

But the funny thing is, I think I already know her. But maybe that's just because she's so nice, intelligent, and when she laughs it's like all the world is suddenly new and exciting.

I like writing this way: just letting the words say what I'm really feeling. It's better than all of psychoanalytic rubbish I normally write. I think I'll give up writing psychoanalytic rubbish.

Sigmund Freud, you're a long-dead duck.

SATURDAY, 13 MAY, AFTERNOON (REVISED WORLD)

Tristan lives in this expensive house in Kew. He meets me at the front door, but instead of showing me in he leads me around the side of the house. "Dad's got some important international clients with him," he explains, "Arabs, I think." A short flight of steps leads downwards to a sort of half-submerged cellar. I step inside, and the creepy feeling is back. I've been here before. Visions of mad dogs barking.

"I have this incredibly strong feeling," I say to Tristan, hesitating in the open doorway. "I've been here before and there was a pack of fierce dogs in here."

"Could only have been one dog," Tristan says. "Lamb Chop."

"That's its name," I say, excited. "Lamb Chop. It was tied up, really fierce. The computer was, was showing toasters."

"He couldn't have been very fierce," Tristan says, looking at me strangely. "He got run over when he was still a puppy. Dad wouldn't have another one, he said his death made me too upset. It did, too."

"That's not what I remember," I say stubbornly, even though I feel stupid. "I remember it as huge, snarling. A, a Rottweiler."

"That's the right breed. Your Mum and Dad must have brought you here when you were about four or five."

That thought also makes me go queasy, and I can't imagine why. The thought of my Mum being here just makes me want to throw up. I say nothing, because there's nothing sensible to say. I sit down on an old couch with the stuffing coming out of one arm, and Tristan perches on a swivel stool in front of his computer. "Tell me everything you can remember," Tristan instructs me.

This seems a bit one-sided. "You've got to tell me everything *you* remember as well."

He nods. "Sure. It's a deal."

"Look, you know how when we met on the ice you told me I was mad?"

"Yeah," says Tristan, "an unintentional pun."

"Well, look, forgive me for saying this. But I've got memories of you saying you were seeing a shrink."

Tristan blushes a deep red, and doesn't say anything for a minute. I'm a bit worried I've touched a raw nerve. Eventually he says in a low, controlled voice, "A psychoanalyst. Her name's Dr. Grogan. I see her twice a week. Tell me more, Jenny. Tell me all you can remember."

"This has got nothing to do with you," I say, "but I've been having these dreams of being rung up on the phone by someone called Rod. He tells me he isn't in our time. He's in 1960."

"I had the same dream," Tristan says wonderingly. "You recorded him on a little tape-recorder and played the tape to me. I remember now. But this is nuts. People can't have the same fantasies in their dreams. That Jungian, not Freudian."

I don't know what he's talking about. "It was real, though, it wasn't a dream. When did it happen? It can't have been very recent, we'd remember it better if it was. But it can't have been years ago either—we'd both have just been tiny."

"Listen, Jenny," Tristan says. He's staring at me as if the most amazing thought he's ever had has just gone off with a bang inside his head. "I think we might be dealing with parallel universes here."

"With *what*? Get a life, Tristan! That only happens on telly."

"No, no, this is serious. There was this Science Show I heard a couple of weeks ago. Paul Davies was yacking on to Michio

Kaku about hyperspace and Many-Worlds cosmology. You know, parallel realities."

"Yeah, I heard that one."

"Davies said you'd go bonkers if you tried to live your life thinking that the universe is branching into stacks of other universes all the time. We have to go around *behaving* as if it's all so simple and straightforward. But really space and time are breeding like rabbits."

"He didn't say *breeding like rabbits*."

"No, but that's what he meant. It's the same with psychology. We can't go around all day long knowing our innermost thoughts are just a chunk of the collective unconscious. We want our thoughts to be our own. But really—"

"Yeah, yeah," I say, shrugging. "Poppa says people don't put much faith in Freud any longer."

"The collective unconscious is Carl Jung, not Sigmund Freud."

He's about to go off on one his favourite rants again. Hastily, I say, "What do you think these different universes have got to do with our funny memories? Aren't they supposed to be in, like, *different universes*?"

"Our memories are leaking over from one world to the other," he insists. "That Rod guy must have something to do with it."

"This is spooky, Tristan," I say, shivering. What he's suggesting is mad, but....

It's actually quite warm in Tristan's secret room under his father's house, but I feel chilly anyway. I'm beginning to believe him. "This is more like something out of *Time Trax* or *The X-Files* than anything Mrs. Levine teaches us about physics."

"But it's interesting, it's exciting," Tristan says. "Can you remember that Rod guy's surname?"

"Why?"

"Because we might be able to track him down, see what he has to say."

"But he was in 1960," I say.

"There are people still alive who were alive in 1960. He'll

just be incredibly old, that's all. He might be sixty or something. Think, Jenny. What was his surname?"

"I don't know," I say miserably.

"Think!"

"*You* think! If I played some tape-recording to you, I must have told you his name."

We both sit in the cellar, thinking. It is an untidy place, full of old books and posters for heavy metal bands. On the computer, a screen saver is endlessly producing bubbles.

"Shouldn't you turn that thing off?" I suggest.

"It's bad for a computer to be turned on and off all the time," Tristan says. "It's better just to let them run."

"Sorry," I mutter, "you've told me that before."

"Have I?"

"Yeah."

"I can't remember," Tristan says.

"I can," I say, "I've got this really strong memory of you saying just that. Really strong."

"Strong!" yells Tristan.

"Not *that* strong," I say.

"No, no, you maroon. The guy on the phone!" Tristan is jumping up and down and swiveling about in his seat.

"How would I know if he's strong or not, I've never seen him," I mumble. I don't like being called a maroon.

"No. That was his *name*. Rod Strong. Rod Strong!"

"No, it wasn't," I say, feeling quite sure of this even if I don't know his real name. "He had an Italian name. He didn't sound Italian, but his parents must have come from there."

"Got it!" yells Tristan. "*Forte*! The Italian for *strong*. Rod Forte, that's gotta be it." The kid is going ape, and I'm starting to get excited myself. Although I know we are not there yet.

"No," I say, "It had more syllables, it was a longer name."

"Well, what else was he called?"

"I'm thinking."

"Well, don't, don't think!"

"What do you mean? *Don't think*? What stupid advice! Don't

you want to know his name?"

"Of course I do," Tristan cries. "But it's an old Freudian trick. If you want to uncover a blocked memory you don't think about the thing itself! You think about something else and the unconscious mind sneaks past the block and *gotcha*! It's all in the *Psychopathology of Everyday Life*. Chapter...er...chapter...I think Three."

"What Mrs. Levine says is," I say, "she says Freud couldn't think straight to save his soul. All his ideas are patriarchal waffle from middle class Vienna before the First World War. She says—"

"Stop raving, girl!" yells Tristan. "How can I think with you going on about this Mrs. Vine and her idiot ideas?"

"Levine...and you're not meant to be thinking about Rod's surname, you said so yourself. So stop cracking on at me about stopping you thinking because...."

"Piano-Forte!"

"What's that got to do with anything?" It's just the proper name for a piano. It means *soft-strong*, from before they had peddles on musical instruments.

"It's his name!" Tristan shrieks. "That's what he was called. Rod Piano-Forte."

"He wasn't a piano," I say, "he had a proper surname, not something stupid."

"Well, what was it?"

I think for a bit, then I say, "You're right, it was very close to *Pianoforte*, but it was...."

"Go on."

"Go-on! That's it!" I yell and suddenly I'm up off the old sofa I'm sitting on and I've embraced Tristan where he's sitting in his chair and I've kissed him and I'm yelling, "Go-on Forte! Go-on Forte! No, that's not right, I remember now, Professor Ram told us about him last weekend at dinner and I didn't even know it was him, God maybe that's why I fainted, I suppose I could just telephone Ram and ask him for the name but that's no good because Ram's gone back to Sydney and I'd have to ask

Poppa for his number and how could I explain why I wanted to, hang on, hang on, he said this Rod had been a student at Sydney university when him and Poppa had been students and he got into some terrible trouble and his name was...Gianforte, Gianforte, Gianforte, Gianforte." I'm giggling like a lunatic. "Quick," I say, "let's go upstairs and get a phone book."

"On the floor next to you." I get the listings open at G and race through them. Giancaspro, Giandzis, Giang Thong, Gianni.

"It's no good," I say, "it would have to be between Giandzis and Giang Thong. He's not in the book. Maybe he's already dead."

"Or moved away," Tristan says.

"We can't go through every phone book in the world, looking for the place he's moved to."

"Internet," Tristan says. To my amazement, he reaches around behind the computer and hooks out a handset. There's a tangle of wires linking it to a jack running into a box that's also connected to the computer.

"You've got a modem?" I cry with strangled envy. This kid has his own line to the Internet! Poppa and Mum would have a cow if I asked for something like that in my room.

"We have to," Tristan says vaguely, holding the phone. "It's a requirement of the school."

"Oh, very class-y," I say sarcastically, but really I'd die for a modem. "What are you doing?"

"We could at least try the capital cities of Australia," Tristan says. "Start with Canberra and then try Sydney."

"That's it, Sydney, he lives in Sydney, Ram said he'd just come back from New Zealand or something. Does the Internet have a Sydney phone book?"

"Probably."

Tristan is keying away like a professional typist. He mutters, "Okay. Sydney area...Gianforte...initial R. Damn, it'd help if we knew his address. Even his suburb. Nope, no R—"

"H!" I gasp, "Initial H. His proper name is Herod or Hotrod or something!"

"Let's try initial H." Tristan clicks, then sends me a smug glance. "Newtown." He is scribbling a number down on a yellow Post-It pad, hands the pad to me. "There you are, Jenny," he says. "Try that."

My fingers are trembling so much that twice I make a hash of punching in the numbers. Finally I do it right, and in my ear I can hear H. Gianforte's phone ringing in New South Wales.

SATURDAY, 13 MAY, AFTERNOON (REVISED WORLD)

Someone picks up the phone and through the STD pips a petulant man's voice says, "Well, what is it this time?"

I'm instantly paralyzed. I peer at Tris, who stares back at me and waves his hands in a questioning way, and I don't know what to say. Is this bad-tempered old man the mysterious "Rod" who's been haunting my dreams? "For heaven's sake," the voice says angrily, "just leave me alone," and I realize with a cold, sinking feeling that he's about to put the phone down in my ear.

"Don't hang up!" I squeal.

"What? Who is this?"

"Please don't hang up," I say, and then my voice gets caught in my throat again.

Tristan is pulling the most hideous faces of frustration at me, as if to say that he would have made a far better fist of this than I'm doing, and it makes me so confused and irritable that I have to turn away from him.

"Why shouldn't I hang up?" the angry old man snaps. "Do I know you? Are you from *Foundations of Physics*?"

"No," I manage to say. "Excuse me, is this Mr. Rod, uh, Gianforte?"

"*Doctor*, damn it, *doctor*! I'll ask you for the last time, who is this?"

"Sir, doctor, please don't hang up, this is very important."

"Is this a child I'm speaking to?" He is intensely suspicious. I've never met anyone as crabby and bad-tempered as this man at the other end of the thousand-kilometer wire between Kew and Newtown. "What's a child doing phoning this number?"

"My name is Genevieve Kane, Dr. Gianforte," I say very carefully and crisply. "Yes, I am a child, well, a teenager, but I'm in the accelerated physics class." I don't know why I've said this, and out of the corner of my eye I see Tristan cover his head with his hands and fall over sideways off the sofa on to the floor. It's enough to give me the giggles, but I clamp down on the merriment because I really don't want to make a mess of this. If I don't find out what's going on with our lives right this moment, the mad scientist will surely never answer another phone call from me as long as he lives.

"Very impressive," Dr. Gianforte is saying sarcastically. "And what possible concern could that be of mine? Besides, how did you obtain my telephone, it's not in the book yet, I've just moved in to this flat. I could sue Telstra for such a lapse of security. Breach of contract!"

"Um, um," I say intelligently, "um, Professor Ram told me you were back in Australia, so I used the Internet directory."

"That's not good enough, I thought I made it plain that I wished the service to be unlisted. Why does nobody pay any attention these days? Ram, you say?" he asks suddenly, interrupting his moaning about the state of the world, "are you referring to Ram Kanthamani?"

"Yes sir," I say, "we had dinner with him the other night."

"But he's at Sydney University," the man says suspiciously. "And you're not, I heard the STD beeps. What sort of game is this?"

I'm getting quite scared by now. The guy sounds like a certified whacko. Tristan has picked himself up off the floor and clunked his stool over beside me, where he's perched with his ear up against the back of the handset. I nudge him away, but he just cozies right back up.

"Actually Professor Ram's recently moved to Melbourne

University," I say. "That's why my father invited him to dinner, we often do that with important people who've just come to Melbourne to work."

"Important? Harrumph!" Dr. Gianforte is indignant. "I don't know how anyone could regard Ram Kanthamani's tedious and derivative work as 'important,' I anticipated everything he's done with quantum theory back in the 1960s, and little good it's done me. Why, if the proper credit had been granted to—"

I take the chance of butting in. "That's just what Professor Ram was saying to my Poppa the other night."

That stops him in his tracks. Still with a suspicious note in his voice, but interested for the first time, the man says, "Oh, is that right? Kanthamani said that?"

I rack my brains, trying to recall just what Ram *had* said. There was that "quantum eraser" parable that seemed to mean that you could change the past, or rather that the past was blurry until it wasn't, or something, but I seem to remember something positive about Rod Gianforte. Oh, yes; it comes back to me.

"He said you knew more about quantum experiments with time than anyone else in this country. He said you could explain Raymond Chiao's recent experiments with, um, with—"

"Yes, yes," the man says impatiently, "delayed quantal photon indeterminacy measures. *How* old did you say you were?"

"Nearly fifteen."

"Good God, and they teach children this sort of theory at that age?"

"No, sir, not exactly. I was just having dinner with—"

And in the middle of my sentence, everything drops into my brain like a load of soggy cold pasta bursting through a brown paper bag. I gasp. I can't breathe. I drop the phone. Everything spins. I topple off the chair. Ripples. Time like ripples. Causes and effects in the wrong order. Changing the past, and changing the future. My brain seems to exist in two worlds at once, like a double exposure. Tristan is leaning over me, helping me sit up, concerned, and I wave him away. He has the phone in his hand, and is speaking with confident clarity to the man at the far end.

I crouch in the middle of the old carpet, and tears are running down my cheeks. Oh, Rod. Poor Rod. I cried when I knew you were going to die, but look what's happened to you now. You didn't die, but you've changed. Time has spared you, and you have ruined your life. You've become a horrible old suspicious meany.

"I don't think she can speak to you just now, sir," Tristan is saying. "She's just had a nasty turn, it might be something she ate. Can we call you back later this—"

I snatch the phone out of his hand and say to the bad-tempered man in Sydney, "Listen, in 1960, thirty-five years ago, you tried to place a call to the future. You built a resonance machine that was connected to the telephone network. Am I right?"

There is a long, appalled silence. "How do you know that? How could anyone— Is Kanthamani spreading this sort of outrageous rumor, after all these years, I simply will not put up with—"

"You got through to me," I tell him.

There is another long pause. The emotion seems to be drained from his voice when he says, "No. Impossible. The machine didn't work. The valves overloaded and caught fire. There was a huge synchrotron surge through the hardware."

"And the computer burned to the ground?" I say, guessing.

"Not just the computer," Rod Gianforte says sadly. "The entire building. It cost half a million pounds to repair the damage."

"In this world," I say, and hold my breath.

His voice regains its abrasive hostility. "What other world is there, you stupid child?"

"The world where you got through to 1995," I explain, holding my temper back, "and you got through to Genevieve Kane, who's me, and we worked out how to make a million dollars through gambling and you set up the Ripple Corporation, and then you—" I can't go on. My head seems full of worms and old, lost grief.

"I what?"

"...You died."

Tristan is staring at me as if I've gone stark, staring mad. But I'm used to that reaction. Maybe it's true.

"The resonance radiation," Rod Gianforte says in a thin, terrible voice. "It would have been massively carcinogenic if I'd kept the original machine running for any length of time. Cancer. How did you know that? How could anyone? Good God, child, even Ram Kanthamani couldn't know that. I've never published...." The wire hums. I hear him grunt, loudly, as if he's been struck a blow to the belly. "Oh God, Genevieve," he says then, "I'm remembering. It's coming across to me. Oh dear Lord, it killed me. It gave me cancer, and it killed me. My double."

I'm sniffling softly as I hear the man at the other end of the phone line weeping for a lost life that never happened because somehow we changed it. Tristan just stands next to me without saying a word, for a change, quietly holding my spare hand very tightly.

Dr. Gianforte sighs, at last, and I can hear him blowing his nose.

"So, it worked. Well. And I'd thought my career had been ruined, when actually I'd avoided dying of cancer. Well."

I whimper, "How come we can remember all this if it didn't happen?"

The man gives a hollow laugh. "A quirk of the quantum universe, Genevieve Kane. I don't suppose you'll understand this yet, not until you've studied the field at university—"

"I want to," I say urgently. "That's what I want to do when I get out of high school. I want to be a physicist."

"Good for you, girlie. It's so strange, I can half remember talking with you...before. I was just a boy myself in those day. Twenty-four, twenty-five."

That doesn't seem too young to me, but I guess for someone who's sixty it must look like that. "Me too," I say. "It's very blurry, though." I glance at Tristan, and suddenly a whole lot of new stuff comes plopping like a heap of poisoned toads into my mind. I jerk away from him and almost drop the phone.

"What, Jenny?"

"Your father!" I spit out at Tristan, feeling really scared and rotten. "Your father and my mother."

I watch it hit him, as if he's recalling something that's repressed from memory, like that Freud stuff he was talking about earlier. He shivers, and looks away from me, embarrassed.

"Well, that hasn't happened, has it?"

"No," I say coldly, "and it's not going to. Your father busted up my parents' marriage."

Tristan is looking awful and sick, but then he stares up at the right-hand corner of the ceiling like you do when you're trying hard to remember something, and after a moment he gives me a snaky look.

"No he didn't, Jenny. I mean, that's a whole different world we're talking about, but he didn't anyway."

"Yes he did," I snarl. I've let the phone drop to my lap, and I'm hunched up in misery. "They got married. Or anyway they were going to."

"But I can remember him telling me, telling that other me, that your Mum had split up with your Dad a year ago. It wasn't his fault, Jen."

I sit absolutely still. It comes back to me like a lesson you've learned and forgotten until the exam, and I cringe even tighter. Tristan's telling the truth. In that other history, my mother hadn't just moved out of their bedroom and upstairs into the spare room. She'd left us completely. She'd gone off and rented her own flat. Tears are leaking down my face again. I pick up the phone and Dr. Gianforte is talking as if he hasn't even noticed I wasn't listening.

"...in a condition of superposition," he says. "I know this is difficult for you to understand, Genevieve, but those two histories haven't properly separated and decohered yet."

"What?" I say, flummoxed. "What?"

"Every time we make an important choice, the quantum universe splits into all the alternatives that would follow from that choice. Say if you came to an intersection and went one way and got hit by a truck, well, in that history you'd be killed. But if you took the other road you'd be all right."

"Like the yellowish photons and bluish photons," I say tiredly.

"I don't follow you."

"It's a parable that Professor Ram told us the other night. You don't know what's happened even after it's happened until after." That doesn't sound right, but I'm too tired and sad and scared to care much.

"Well, that's a very vague way to put it, Genevieve," Rod Gianforte says, "but you're on the right track. You see, we've done something very peculiar here. In a way, we've short-circuited the universe. Correction: the universes."

"There's more than one universe?" I raise my eyebrows at Tristan, who's trying with great difficulty to overhear our conversation.

"There is now. In that other history, I opened up a reso-nance pathway from 1960 to 1995. But it killed me, which sort of cross-wired everything and all the fuses of that spacetime loop burned out. It's as if history started again from some point before I made contact with you. But the different quantum states stayed entangled. Somehow we've welded the two together. There's been some discussion about this possibility by a British physicist called David Deutsch. He believes that—"

"Excuse me," I say. "I don't understand much of this. Could you try to keep it real simple?"

Some of his bad temper comes back. "Oh. Very well. I thought you were a clever child."

"Yes," I tell him, "I've got a mind like a steel trap." A new shiver runs down my spine.

Tristan says, "Ask him if he's built a replacement machine."

"Okay. Uh, doctor, did you try it again after the machine blew up?"

He laughs harshly. "Hardly. I was lucky to escape with any of my professional reputation intact. Besides, I concluded that it couldn't be done with the available technology."

I look at the neat little Apple computer on the desk. Toasters have started flapping across its screen. "That was then," I tell him. "What about now?"

"Don't think I haven't thought about it. It's all I've worked on for the last thirty years—in my spare time, of course, after I'd corrected a hundred stupid essays every night." He sounds exasperated, and I guess I can't blame him. "In fact, with today's micro-technology, and Deutsch's advances in theory, I suspect we're only a decade or so away from a safe, functioning temporal resonance system."

"Oh." I'm disappointed. "You reckon if you tried to build a resonator now it'd just blow up again?"

"No, I imagine we've got that under control with micro-circuitry. It's the radiation effects I'm thinking of. Give it ten years and we could have a shielded machine that dials *back* in time to a specific number—and then we'd really see some fancy effects."

I stare at Tristan with my mouth open. "He says he could get one that sends messages backwards as well as forwards."

Tris jumps up, rubbing his hands together. "That way you could win the lottery every week! You could change history!"

"Listen, Dr. Gianforte, why don't you get in touch with Professor Kanthamani and tell him about all this? He might get you a lab to work in, and—"

"I'm too damned old," says the voice from Sydney. He really does sound old, too, even though he's not all that much older than Poppa, now that I stop to think about it. "Too old and bitter and twisted, child. I've had my innings, and my score has not been impressive." I hear a thin, angry laugh come down the line. "In either history. Dead in one, a disappointed old misanthrope in the other. I shall leave it to someone else to carry on my work, Genevieve."

"I could do it!" I blurt. Suddenly I don't want him just to hang up and go out of my life. I can't really recall that other life in any detail, but there's a distant warm memory of a bright, caring man who died thirty-five years ago, and somehow this poor sad man is all I have left of that memory. Besides, I can't bear to imagine that his work will simply be lost, even if it is rediscovered by some nameless researcher in the twenty-first century. "I'll go to university and carry on your work," I tell him urgently.

There is another long silence, but I don't get any angry vibes down the line. After a time, Dr. Gianforte says in a pleased voice, "Well, perhaps you could, young Genevieve. I have all my research material stored here in my computer—"

"Print it out and mail it to me," I suggest. "I could hang on to it until I know enough physics to pick up your trail, and then—"

"Print what?" Tristan says. "Mail what?"

"He could send me everything he's got in his computer."

"Just put it on disk," Tristan says.

I'm crushed. "Oh, of course." I speak into the phone. "You could send me a Mac computer disk. For that matter, you could email your files to my father's computer. Do you want his number?"

"That's possible in principle," Dr. Gianforte muses, "except that we're talking about a couple of megabytes of text files and twenty or thirty megs of instrument data, so he'd need access to a Syquest drive. Hmm. In any case, of course, I'd have to ring him first and ask his permission, and that would lead to endless complications, and I'd have to get Ram to vouch for me.... No, really, it's just too much trouble. Let's forget the whole thing. I'm sick of it. Sick of it."

Tristan is pulling at my arm. "Use my modem right now. Ask him if he's got an Internet site. If he'll tell us his Net address—"

"Brilliant," I squeal. Eagerly, I explain our idea.

"You have a computer there? Why didn't you say so? Are you on the Net?"

Tristan nods. "I have a CompuServe account."

"Very well," Dr. Gianforte says. "You can find my research material under the name 'quanttime,' I've arranged it for anybody in the physics community who cares to study my findings and attempt a replication. Not that anyone with a brain in their head has bothered accessing it." He pauses. "Er, look, I know I was rather gruff with you when you first called...."

"That's all right," I tell him. The memory of that other, younger Rod helps to ease the sting of how rude he was.

"Well, it's not really all right. I'm a bad-tempered old stick, and my personal unhappiness is no excuse. I just want to thank you for taking the trouble to call me. You've given me a new lease on life. Who knows, perhaps I'll get back to this resonance research after all. If not, I expect you to finish it for me in the fullness of time. Is that a deal?"

"Deal," I say, grinning. "It's been a pleasure doing business with you." My voice drops, and I say quietly, "I'm glad you didn't die, Dr. Gianforte."

"Perhaps I am, too. And by the way, girlie?"

I hate the expression "girlie," it makes my scalp itch. But I can tell he's trying to be nice.

"Yes?"

"Call me Rod."

"Thanks, Rod. Call me Jenny."

I hang up. Tris starts scrolling through directory menus. Dr. Gianforte's Home Page comes up on the screen. It's the bare minimum, no fancy graphics or user-friendly icons, but it looks as if we should be able to find our way through it with a bit of effort. He finds a folder called "quanttime," utters a little cry of triumph, and clicks on it. After a few minutes, we realize that it's all heavy philosophy and even heavier mathematics that neither of us can understand—yet. Dr. Rod is right, this is going to be a long-term project. Tristan puts an electronic bookmark on Dr. Gianforte's site, so we can get back to it easily next time, logs off, and we get up and stretch and go out into the garden.

The ornamental pond is just where I "remember" it. A tall man is standing near a weeping willow, tearing up bread crusts and throwing them to the birds. He turns as we walk on to the grass, and my heart turns over. Thring!

"Hello, Tris," he says in quite a nice posh voice. "And who is your friend?"

"Dad." Tristan clearly likes his father. He touches his arm and gestures to me. "Jenny Kane, meet my father. Her dad's an economist at the university."

"Oh yes, Dr. Kane, we've met once or twice. And your charming mother Harriet. I hope they're well?"

My stomach sinks even further at the mention of my mother's name. But the man does not seem to be hiding any deep dark secrets. That was a different history, I tell myself, and we're going to keep it that way.

"Yes, sir," I say uncomfortably. Looking for something neutral to say, I mumble, "I like your garden."

"Beautiful, isn't it?" He glances in a rather touching way at the autumn landscape, the birds moving slowly on the blue-gray surface of the water. "My late wife designed all this. She had a special eye for beauty." He gives himself a shake, and I decide he's not such a bad old stick. "Well, very nice to meet you, Jenny. Perhaps Tristan will invite you to join us for tea, if your parents will allow that?"

I nod without saying anything, and a phone rings loudly. Both Tris and I look in surprise back toward the den, but the ringing is coming from his father's belt. Snatching up his mobile phone, and waving farewell to us with his other hand, Tristan's father turns toward the house, barking into the phone: "Thring!"

I just break up. I can't help myself.

Everything collapses in on itself. I'm almost paralyzed with laughter, red-faced and humiliated, laughing like a nut case. Edward Thring pays no attention, disappearing into the big house. Tristan stares at me in astonishment, and I gasp and shriek with mirth. And I can't explain it to him. I can't scream out, "Thring! Thring!" And I don't really know why I wish to. It's just all so incredibly funny.

Through my laughter, I hear a phone ringing. It sets me laughing even harder, and then after a while Tristan is shaking my arm.

"Pull yourself together, Jenny, there's a phone call for you."

"What? What? Where?"

"My phone."

"Rod again? Maybe he wants to know if we found his site—"

"No. This is someone else."

How could it be? Nobody even knows I'm here. Poppa and Mum certainly don't. Anyway, wouldn't they ring the main house? Maybe Maddy copied it down when we all swapped numbers at the skating rink. But why should she phone me at Tris's? Unless she's after him. Maybe she's sick of David. I give him a dark scowl as we trot back down the path to his den. The phone is lying on his desk beside the computer.

"Hello?"

A woman's voice says, "Don't hang up!"

Another little jolt, like electricity, goes through me, making my hands and feet prickle. What does that remind me of? I don't know the young woman's voice, but strangely enough it sounds a bit like Poppa. His accent, I mean; he's got quite a deep voice. Or maybe it's Mum's voice I'm reminded of.

"I won't hang up," I say. "Why should I?"

"Just don't. You might not believe this."

I start to get it, then. And I find this big huge grin spreading across my face.

"It worked?"

There's a gust of happy laughter at the other end of the phone. "It sure did! Only took eighteen years, too."

Tristan is jittering from one foot to the other, like a little kid who has to go urgently and needs the teacher's permission to leave the room. Except I'm sure that leaving the room is the last thing Tris has on his mind.

"Who is it?" he hisses. "*What* worked?"

"It's a person called....Jenny," I tell him, grinning fit to bust.

There's another gust of laughter from the other end. "Show some respect for your elders, Jenny! It's *doctor*, as our friend Rod Gianforte insists. Dr. Genevieve Kane speaking."

Tristan is no slouch. He's gazing at me and at the phone in astonished delight. "It's...*you*?"

"Yep," I say. "In 19— Uh, Genevieve, what year is that?"

"2013, Jenny," the confident voice tells me. "Ask Tris if he'd be so kind as to buzz off and make you both a hot chocolate, then pull up a chair. We have some catching up to do, kiddo."

"I'll leave you two alone," Tristan says, rolling his eyes heaven-ward. "If there's one thing I can't stand, it's a long session of girl-talk." Then that mad boy reaches across in front of me, pulls an egg from my ear, snaps it on the desk, peels it, and is popping it in his mouth as he closes the cellar door behind him.

ABOUT THE AUTHORS

DAMIEN BRODERICK met up with **RORY BARNES** (who'd learned to walk and talk in a tribal mud hut in Northern Rhodesia) more than forty years ago at Australia's Monash University. They shared various student houses with a motley crew of would-be writers who did what students did in the '60s: got pissed, screwed around, smoked some pot, engaged in a small amount of semi-violent protest and wrote a lot of essays. Broderick sold some stories and books and eventually got a Ph.D., Barnes did some teaching then wandered around Southeast Asia and the Middle East. Since 1983, they have co-authored seven novels. Barnes and his two sons live in Adelaide, South Australia. Broderick shares several houses with his American wife Barbara in San Antonio, Texas. They are both far more law-abiding than their raffish hero, to their regret.

www.ingramcontent.com/pod-product-compliance
Lightning Source LLC
Chambersburg PA
CBHW022151260626
47155CB00017B/1721